"Can you breathe?" she asked.

Oh, yeah, he could breathe, and right now he smelled a woman fresh from the shower, still warm from the heat of the water, scented with soap and shampoo. Even in the light from that single lantern and the flashlight on the floor he could tell her skin was flushed a healthy pink.

And in that instant he wanted her so much that he gripped the damp towels in his hands until his fingers ached.

"Yeah," he managed to say, aware that his voice sounded oddly thick. He cleared his throat and looked away before he could make a fool of himself. "Yeah," he said again, more firmly, even though he was lying because right now it felt like there wasn't any air left in the room, or in the entire universe. Primitive rhythms beat in his blood, in his loins.

Dear Reader,

No Ordinary Hero was an adventure for me, a twist on the usual suspense. I left a question dangling at the end, hoping you would choose whichever answer best pleases you.

When two people fall in love, they often encounter differences in the way they view things, and the process by which they come to agree, or at least agree to disagree, has always fascinated me.

None of us would want to fall in love with a mirror image. How boring that would make life, to live in an echo chamber, and never experience the magic of someone else's way of seeing even mundane things.

Mike and Del face a few major hurdles because they come from such different cultural backgrounds. Love, however, is not about to leave them alone in their private worlds.

Nor is the house.

Best,

Rachel Lee

RACHEL LEE

No Ordinary Hero

ROMANTIC
SUSPENSE

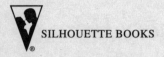 SILHOUETTE BOOKS

Recycling programs
for this product may
not exist in your area.

ISBN-13: 978-0-373-27713-1

NO ORDINARY HERO

Visit Silhouette Books at www.eHarlequin.com

Printed in U.S.A.

Books by Rachel Lee

Silhouette Romantic Suspense

An Officer and a Gentleman #370
Serious Risks #394
Defying Gravity #430
★Exile's End #449
★Cherokee Thunder #463
★Miss Emmaline and the Archangel #482
★Iron Heart #494
★Lost Warriors #535
★Point of No Return #566
★A Question of Justice #613
★Nighthawk #781
★Cowboy Comes Home #865
★Involuntary Daddy #955
Holiday Heroes #1487
★★A Soldier's Homecoming #1519
★★Protector of One #1555
★★The Unexpected Hero #1567
★★The Man from Nowhere #1595
★★Her Hero in Hiding #1611
★★A Soldier's Redemption #1635
★★No Ordinary Hero #1643

★Conard County
★★Conard County: The Next Generation

Silhouette Shadows

Imminent Thunder #10
★Thunder Mountain #37

Silhouette Books

★A Conard County Reckoning
★Conard County
The Heart's Command
  "Dream Marine"

Montana Mavericks

Cowboy Cop #12

World's Most Eligible
  Bachelors

★The Catch of Conard County

RACHEL LEE

was hooked on writing by the age of twelve, and practiced her craft as she moved from place to place all over the United States. This *New York Times* bestselling author now resides in Florida and has the joy of writing full-time.

Her bestselling Conard County series (see www.conardcounty.com) has won the hearts of readers worldwide, and it's no wonder, given her own approach to life and love. As she says, "Life is the biggest romantic adventure of all—and if you're open and aware, the most marvelous things are just waiting to be discovered." Readers can email Rachel at RachelLee@ConradCounty.com.

For my oldest daughter, for whom every day is a battle and every night another triumph.

Chapter 1

Mike Windwalker, D.V.M., came home early from work, pulling into his driveway in his battered brown van, practically a veterinary clinic on wheels. It had been a busy but short day, allowing him to leave his assistants in charge of the kennels and point himself toward a relaxing late afternoon and evening.

A well-earned bit of relaxation, considering he rarely enjoyed a day off. Not that he minded his workload. In fact he loved it because it gave him scant time to think about all the things missing in his life. And the animals he spent his time with, if not all of their owners, didn't give a damn that he was a "redskin," a full-blooded Cheyenne, an escapee from the rez.

He climbed out of the van, feeling a little stiff from an unusual encounter that morning with a bovine. The animal had been half insane but worth enough money that the rancher wanted to be sure there wasn't some treatment for the steer. In the process, he'd been kicked, although not too badly, nearly bitten—thank God he'd dodged that one—and had wrestled with twelve hundred pounds of maddened muscle while trying to get a blood sample.

He'd guessed it was rabies to begin with, but the rancher had been insistent. In the end, however, he'd simply had to put the animal down, over strenuous objections, with the flat statement that he wasn't going to risk his own life or anyone else's when the diagnosis was damn near written all over the steer.

He'd left with the body of the steer and dropped it off in his cooler so that tomorrow he could remove the brain and spinal cord to send to the state lab.

Fun day, stubborn client, and now he ached all over. Yet he still felt a lot of sympathy for the rancher, who, like most in his business, was running on a margin so small that losing one steer, just one, could be a terrifying prospect.

The only thing that had made the guy stand back and let Mike put the animal down was the possibility that if he kept that steer around, he might wind up with a sick herd—the only catastrophe worse than losing a single animal.

Mike tossed his head, causing his inky hair to fall back from his face. Despite local opinions about Native Americans, he defiantly wore his hair long. Let 'em stare. His heritage was stamped on his face, and his hair was the crowning glory. Usually he tied it back with a beaded band, but today when he left work, he'd discarded the band. His scalp was grateful.

"Hi, Dr. Windwalker!"

The light, youthful voice called to him from the

house next door, and he turned to see Colleen Carmody sitting in her wheelchair on the large front porch. The Carmodys had moved in a little over a month ago, and he'd shared a few brief conversations with thirteen-year-old Colleen, who was incurably cheerful and friendly. He'd even spoken to her mother Delia, or Del, a few times, but he tried to keep the contact to a minimum. He didn't want any trouble, and he certainly didn't want to cause any to the Carmodys. He knew his place; it had been beaten into him.

"You're home early," Colleen said with a wide, welcoming smile.

He couldn't be rude to that girl, not for anybody's sake. From inside the house he heard a banging, indicating that Colleen's mother was busy at the restoration work she did to support herself and her daughter. "Yeah," he replied, without approaching. "And I need it. I had a hard morning."

"What happened?" Colleen asked.

"A very sick steer would have liked to kill me. I didn't let him, but he almost won the fight."

The girl giggled, a delightful sound, and rolled her chair across the porch so she was a little closer. Her red hair caught some of the spring sunlight that filtered through the leaves before it crept under the porch roof, and flamed. "You don't look like you did so bad."

"That's because my bruises are under my pants. I figure I'll look like a piece of modern art in a day or two."

Another giggle answered him.

"How's your day been?" he asked. Nope, no way could he be rude to that child.

He watched, feeling a twinge of concern as he saw

the girl's smile vanish. "Colleen?" Something must be wrong.

"It's nothing," the girl said. "I just don't like this house."

"Why not?"

She hesitated, then said in a rush, "I feel like there's something else in there. I hear things. It's creepy!"

He looked from her to the two-story, clapboard house, and the blank eyes of the windows. Old house. Plenty of rot, no doubt, and maybe raccoons or mice. But something else... Some feeling he tried to shove away, because at least around here he had to be one hundred percent a man of science and bury instincts honed throughout his youth by people who believed in spirits and the sentience of even the very rocks.

"Rats?" he suggested. "Raccoons?"

"Mom checked. That's what she thinks it is."

He nodded, his gaze returning to the child. "She's probably right. But you don't think so?"

Colleen shrugged. "She didn't find anything."

"Ah." He tried a small smile. "Then maybe some mice got into the walls. They can be so hard to find once they do that."

"Yeah. That's what Mom said, too." Colleen gave another small shrug, seeming a bit embarrassed now. "I know she's probably right, but it's creepy anyway. Especially late at night."

"That would creep me out, too," he said sympathetically, letting his barriers down just a shade. "Scratching and banging from something you can't see... Nah, I wouldn't like that either."

That elicited a smile from Colleen. "You're kinda okay, Dr. Windwalker."

"Just call me Mike." He was about to say goodbye and head into his own house when the screen door behind Colleen squeaked open and a woman poked her head out.

"Colleen? Did you call me?" Then, as she saw Mike, "Oh! Hi, Dr. Windwalker."

"Just Mike." He felt nearly embarrassed that he'd kept such a distance since they moved in that they didn't even feel free to call him by his first name. Of course, he was only protecting himself and them.

Del Carmody stepped out onto the porch with a smile. And once again he felt the impact of her beauty. Black Irish to the bone, she didn't have her daughter's flaming hair but instead hair much like his, the color of a raven's wing, only shinier and finer. The impact was heightened by intense blue eyes and milky Irish skin. Right now she looked a little dusty, but that didn't detract one iota from a body that even in jeans and a loose work shirt sans sleeves showed a perfect shape, the kind of shape only a woman could achieve from hard physical labor. The kind of shape that had always drawn him, more muscular than average but still curved in all the right ways. And that smile of hers.

Things he really shouldn't notice. Couldn't afford to notice. But he saw them all anyway.

"Mike," she acknowledged, still smiling. "Didn't mean to interrupt you guys, but I heard Colleen's voice and wondered if she needed something."

"I was just telling Doctor…I mean Mike, about the mice in the house."

"The noises." Del nodded, looking at her daughter with a flicker of concern. Clearly she cared that her daughter was frightened, even if the explanation had to be utterly benign. A loving mother.

"Mice in the walls can be a beast to get rid of," he volunteered.

"Tell me about it," Del said. She came farther onto the porch and leaned against the railing. "That's where they must be because I can't find any sign of them in the attic. I just hope I can get rid of them before one dies inside a wall."

"That'll make the place uninhabitable for a while," he agreed. He felt awkward, standing so far away in his driveway, knowing the neighborly thing would be to approach. But he didn't approach white folks readily anymore. Hadn't since he was eighteen. If they came to him in a friendly fashion, fine. But he never made the first overture. And this situation, with a widow and her daughter, could cause exactly the kind of mess he'd been avoiding his entire adult life.

Awkward to stand at a distance, even more awkward to just walk away. Needless rudeness did him no favors, but then neither did unwanted friendliness. He'd given up sighing over reality years ago, though. The West was the West, and people here still harbored old hatreds.

He didn't feel sorry for himself. Others, he believed, had it far worse. But he was well aware that he was always on a tightrope, at least in this part of the country. It hadn't been so bad back east where he'd gone to veterinary school, but here…memories were long. On both sides, if he were to be honest about it.

"I hope that all my sawing and banging isn't driving you nuts," Del said.

He allowed himself a faint smile. "Not at all. I'm

usually at work during the hours you're banging away. How's it going?"

"Well, the place was in worse shape than I guessed when I looked it over before I bought it. A lot of hidden problems. But it's coming along."

"A lot of rot?"

Her blue eyes met his openly, tired but smiling. "Oh, of course. Worse than I anticipated. When I started pulling out the old plaster, I found some of the studs were in pretty bad shape, and the lath behind the plaster isn't so great either."

"It's a shame you have to replace the plaster at all."

"I know." She turned toward him, facing him. An open posture. "They don't build them like that anymore. It's killing me to have to put in drywall, but plastering would be a bigger headache than I want to buy, especially since I may have to replace all of it. I guess the roof must have leaked into the walls at some point, for a long time." She looked back at the house and then smiled at him. "This job is always an adventure."

"So's Mike's," Colleen offered. "A steer tried to kill him."

Del's eyebrows, perfectly arched, lifted. "Why in the world would a steer do that?"

"I'm pretty sure he was rabid. He got in a few kicks, but I dodged well enough that the damage is minor."

Colleen giggled. "He said he's going to look like modern art."

Del's smile widened and she chuckled. "Ouch. There are days that leave me looking that way, too."

He turned his mind away from inevitable thoughts about what might lie under her clothing, bruised and unbruised.

"How would a steer become rabid?" Del asked.

"The same way you or I could. A bite from an infected animal. I'll look for the marks when I start the necropsy tomorrow, but it could have been anything from a raccoon to a wolf."

Colleen spoke. "I bet the rancher thinks it was a wolf. They hate the wolves."

"Yes, they do." And entirely too much so, though Mike could understand their reasoning. For his own part, he prized the return of wolves to the area, both culturally and scientifically. "But it could have been something else. A rabid animal will bite just about anything regardless of size. And it's my job to find out."

"I hope it was a bat or something else," Colleen said. "I like wolves."

"I do, too." Really. Because if he found a wolf bite on the animal, there might well be other infected wolves, and the hunt would begin. Considering that as near as anyone could tell there was still only a single pack on Thunder Mountain, that would be a tragedy, both for the wolves and the ecology.

Del straightened a bit. "You must be tired," she said to him. "Don't let us keep you in your driveway."

She smiled, but instead of feeling grateful for her concern, he felt dismissed. "Thanks," he said, trying to keep a pleasant tone. "Nice chatting." Then he turned and started toward his door.

And on his back he could feel the eyes of two white women, forbidden territory.

Del watched Mike Windwalker stride away to his door, thinking he was an extremely attractive man, from his face to those narrow hips cased in worn denim. And she liked the coppery color of his skin, such a contrast to her own ghastly paleness. All her life she wished she could tan rather than freckle. Ah, well, she wasn't in the market for a man, any man.

Then she looked down at her daughter. "You getting hungry?"

"Could be." Colleen grinned.

"How hungry?"

"Um…" Colleen pretended to think it over. "Just teensy hungry right now. Big hungry comes later."

"Fair enough." She reached for the grips on the back of the wheelchair and heard an immediate protest.

"Mom! I can do it myself."

Del had to smile. Colleen's independence and upbeat attitude always made her smile…except when it made her cry for what her daughter had lost. "Okay, okay. I'll just get the door."

"I want chips!"

"Whole-grain pretzels."

"Sheesh, Mom, I have a growing brain. I need the fat."

"Smarty pants."

"I learned it in biology."

"You learn too much in biology."

In the kitchen, which was still awaiting renovations, the dust layered everything. No way to avoid it at this stage of restoration, so Del grabbed a wet rag and wiped down just enough of it to feed her daughter some pretzels without all the plaster dust. In other parts of the house, near open windows, big fans tried to suck dust out of the house. They helped but not entirely. Just as the plastic she hung over the door to the kitchen didn't completely prevent the dust from getting in.

As she was wiping around the sink, she noticed the window beside it was unlocked. She paused, wondering how that had happened. She never opened the windows in here because she didn't want to create a draft that would suck the dust in around the edges of the plastic.

Damn, she couldn't remember. For all she knew it had been unlocked for weeks or more. She might have done it in the way she did so many things, while thinking of something else. Except, she wouldn't have closed it without locking it again, would she?

Hell. As forgetful as she seemed to be getting lately, it was silly even to wonder about it. Maybe one of the workmen or deliverymen had opened it briefly.

Sighing, she reached out to flip the lock closed.

"What do you want to drink?" she asked after she'd put a couple of large pretzels on a plate.

"Soda."

Del faced her daughter. "You do this to drive me crazy, right?"

Colleen giggled. "No." But the way she giggled had given lie to her denial.

Del laughed herself. "You know what's in the fridge."

"Yeah. Darn it. Wouldn't you know I'd have a health freak for a mom?"

"Such a curse." But Del couldn't help feeling a pang. Her daughter wanted the same simple things every other kid her age wanted. Having to take extra care about her weight because her activities were limited only made it harder for both of them. "Okay," she said. "Tell you what. I'll get some diet soda at the store next time. Will that do?"

"I'll love you forever." An impish smile. "Can I have cranberry juice?"

"Always." Del pulled a bottle of low-calorie juice from the fridge, rinsed a glass to remove any dust, filled it and handed it to Colleen. "Dr. Windwalker seems really nice."

Before Colleen could answer, there was a buzz that sounded almost like laughter, and the girl pulled out her cell phone. "Yeah," she answered absently as she scanned the screen then started rapidly texting a reply. The tap-tap of the keys was a counterpoint to every waking moment of the day. "Can I go over to Mary Jo's for a sleepover tomorrow?"

"Sure, once I clear it with her mom." Colleen had adapted amazingly well to her disability—so well that Del wondered if some of it weren't just show to protect her mother—and the parents of her friends were more than ready to do the extra care Colleen required. Mary Jo's mom had even installed handicap bars in her bathroom. But Del always felt she had to clear it.

"Mary Jo says her mom says to stop worrying about it."

That sounded like Beth Andrews, for certain. "Okay, but tell Mary Jo to tell her mom to call me anyway."

"Sheesh." The word was accompanied by a small frown as the tapping resumed. "Okay, she'll call." Colleen looked up. "I guess I need to go back outside?"

"Just for a bit, sweetie. I'm done making dust for the day, but I want to get rid of some more of it and let the rest settle safely."

Colleen had a little flip tray on her wheelchair and she

had set the pretzels on it. The drink created a problem, however.

Del didn't wait for the question. "Why don't I carry your food out while you resume the neighborhood watch?"

That at least earned another laugh. Unfortunately, with all the dust, and later with the chemicals she would need to use for stripping and varnishing, it was best if Colleen remained outside as much as possible. Colleen didn't seem to mind—texting seemed to be her major absorption, and sometimes friends came over to gather on the front porch with popcorn and beverages. Three days a week she went to physical therapy. School also occupied a good deal of her time except over the summers, and Del hoped to have the messiest of the work done on this house before school let out.

After she settled Colleen on the porch, she went back inside to get out her shop vacuum and start cleaning up as much as she could. Because it was still late spring, the afternoon would start getting chilly soon, and she wanted Colleen to come inside before it did.

Back inside with the inexplicable scratchings and bangings. Those concerned her. At first when Colleen had mentioned them, Del had assumed there were vermin in the attic and hadn't been too troubled. But now, having checked everywhere she could and never having heard the sounds herself, she worried about more than vermin.

She worried about why Colleen might imagine such sounds. Worried about whether she needed to mention them to Colleen's doctor or wait a little longer to see what developed.

At the back of her mind, she never quite escaped the

feeling that another shoe was about to drop. Maybe it was just because once the worst happened to you, you never felt entirely safe again. And losing her husband and having her daughter paralyzed by an auto accident had been pretty much the worst she ever wanted to imagine.

But there was also the sense that Colleen had adapted too well and too quickly to losing the use of her legs. Oh, at first there had been plenty of tears and despair, many cries of "I wish I could have died, too." But in a matter of just a month or so, those feelings seemed to have evaporated, leaving an unexpectedly cheerful and uncomplaining daughter.

Del kept thinking that at least once in a while Colleen ought to complain about *something*. But the child never did. At least not around her. Another concern. She didn't want Colleen to feel as if she had to hide negative feelings from her, that she had to be strong for her mom. That would be an unfair and heavy burden for any child that age, including Colleen.

And then, sometimes she even worried about *herself*. Because while Colleen might be hearing sounds, Del herself seemed to be becoming a bit too forgetful, and maybe even imaginative. A couple of times in the past few weeks she'd come home after leaving the house empty to find things out of place. At least she *thought* they were out of place. And each time she had the distinct impression someone had been *in* the house.

Which was utterly insane, because she locked the place up tight every single time she and Colleen went out. There were simply too many valuable tools and construction supplies lying around to take any chance.

So she had to be forgetting where she left stuff. Not a good sign, but probably not all that abnormal either.

Del sighed heavily, pulled on her dust mask and picked up the hose to vacuum the living room she'd been working on. One room at a time to try to keep the mess under control. Damn dust still managed to seep everywhere.

Flipping houses had been a good idea overall after the accident that took Don and disabled Colleen. With the life insurance money, she'd been able to buy a fixer-upper, and with the skills learned growing up on a farm, studying architectural engineering in college, and some heavy-duty studying to fill the gaps, she'd learned most of the trades necessary to turn a mess into a desirable property. Things had gone well, mostly, although at the moment she still had one property she hadn't been able to sell in this belt-tightening time, or even to rent to someone.

But her bank account was still healthy enough, and living in the houses she worked on made the expense easier to bear. This week, however, she'd need the electrician, as well as a plumber to help with the downstairs bath she intended to add. Those would be big bills, but necessary to ensure the house was up to code. At the moment it most certainly was not.

Living in the house she was working on also made it possible to keep an eye on Colleen. She couldn't have the girl in one house while she worked on another, and her aunt Sally wasn't up to taking full responsibility. Yes, Aunt Sally helped out when needed, especially at times when Del needed to be away to purchase materials, but Sally was getting up in years and at best could only keep an eye on Colleen and make sure she got decent meals.

Although even the need for Sally's help was beginning to pass. Colleen had learned tricks for getting herself in and out of bed, getting up off the floor if she fell for some reason, and she could even manage to cook a little, though that was difficult in a kitchen that wasn't designed for someone in a chair. And in a worst-case scenario, Colleen always had her phone within a couple of inches.

Still, Del worried. How could she not? She didn't want Colleen to have another bad experience of some kind, and total independence still lay in the future.

As she vacuumed the dust that coated the living room after a day spent pulling out damaged plaster, she chewed her lip behind her mask and tried to tell herself that everything would work out for Colleen in time.

She had to believe that.

Then her thoughts drifted back to Mike Windwalker. He was a reserved guy. She'd already noted that he didn't seem inclined to chat for long with neighbors. Shy? Maybe.

But, Lord, he was good-looking. Male eye candy, and she didn't usually respond to that. Or maybe it had just been so long since she'd been with a man that her libido was acting up.

The thought made her chuckle quietly. Well, if it had to act up, it had chosen a great object for attention. She could watch that man walk up his driveway any day.

And maybe, with a tiny bit of effort, she could break through that reserve and get to know him a bit. She liked to know her neighbors, especially now. It made her feel safer, and certainly safer for Colleen.

A thought suddenly occurred to her, and she switched off the vacuum for a minute. Maybe it was the confluence of her thoughts, but Colleen had recently asked for a kitten. Who better to ask about getting one than the local vet who lived next door?

And maybe a kitten would make Colleen feel safer from those scratchings she heard. Certainly it wouldn't hurt to find out if a cat could help with mice in the walls...if indeed there were mice.

Finally she switched the vacuum on again and resumed her task. A cat might be the answer to a number of things.

Or not.

She made up her mind to talk to Mike Windwalker about it soon. A cat, or maybe a small dog, depending on what he thought might handle small vermin better. But nothing too big, given Colleen's paralysis. Something small and cuddly that would chase away the mice.

Because either there were mice in these walls or something worrisome was happening to Colleen.

And the latter was an idea she refused to entertain.

Chapter 2

Del loved Saturday mornings because she put aside her work and devoted her full attention to Colleen. Yes, they usually had errands to run, things like grocery shopping, but it was still time spent together without the intervention of work or school. Sometimes, like today, they even took in a matinee at the movies.

Today they had gone to see a silly animated film that had made them laugh heartily, and then afterward she had dropped Colleen at Mary Jo's for the night.

Sunday was always a day off, too, for her at least, but there was church in the morning, and the inevitable socializing that went with it after the service, and then Colleen usually spent the afternoon on schoolwork. Often, by then, Del felt tired enough to need a nap.

So Saturdays were a special time for them both: no school, no work, no therapists.

This Saturday, however, as she drove home from

dropping Colleen at Mary Jo's, Del realized she felt reluctant to go home. She tried to tell herself not to be ridiculous, that these brief times to herself without work should be prized, and that she deserved the break as much as Colleen deserved to have fun with her friends at a sleepover.

But a weird kind of edginess troubled her anyway in the waning afternoon light. She couldn't put her finger on the source, and she finally decided that she must have forgotten to do something and would remember it later.

As she turned into her driveway and stopped the car, she looked up at the house and felt a totally inexplicable impulse to just drive away.

Now that was crazy! Had Colleen's talk of noises gotten to her?

She made herself climb out of the car, but still she hesitated. Not very long, thank goodness, because she heard another vehicle and turned to see Mike Windwalker pulling up next door. She waved, trying to smile in a friendly fashion, and he nodded to her as he braked then switched off his truck.

The usual thing would be for her to continue into her house. She'd greeted him, so she didn't have to remain outside. But something pushed her across the ragged, patchy lawn toward him.

He climbed out of his vehicle, wearing a dark blue chambray shirt and jeans, not very different from what she wore, and she thought that an instant of surprise passed over his strong features. If so, it vanished quickly.

"Hi," he said as she approached.

She heard an odd note of caution in his tone, couldn't

figure it out, but it didn't matter anyway because she was already committed. She'd started closing the distance between them and now couldn't simply turn away.

"Hi," she said. Now what? She couldn't exactly tell him that for some reason she didn't want to go into her house. Then she remembered the kitten question. "Can I ask you something? If you'd rather I make an appointment, I'll understand." She gave an uneasy laugh. "Asking for a neighbor's professional opinion for free is something I usually avoid."

A slow smile dawned on his face. God, he was good-looking. "I don't mind. You never know when I might have a professional question for you."

She gave another laugh. "Fair enough. Colleen's been asking for a kitten. And I got to thinking yesterday, what with the possibility of mice in the walls, that might not be a bad thing. Then I wondered if a small dog would be better."

He leaned back against his van, folding his arms, and in the process thrust his hips forward. Oh, she didn't want to notice those narrow hips again. She dragged her gaze back to his face.

"That depends," he said easily. Apparently on familiar ground, he felt comfortable. She could identify with that, since she was definitely *off* comfortable ground herself right now. "What would be easiest for you? There are some good small dogs that would take care of mice and rats, but dogs need more attention than cats. Walks and so on. On the other hand, not every cat is a good mouser."

"Really?" That surprised her.

"Really. It depends a lot on how the kitten is raised. Most learn to hunt from their mothers, whereas with some dogs, you've got a strong inbred instinct and territoriality."

"I didn't know that!"

"Most people don't. If you really want a good mouser, I can check around the local ranches for a barn cat, but that's more likely to be less a pet than a hunter."

Del sighed. "I had no idea this could be so complicated."

A quiet laugh escaped him. "You're not alone. Just ask yourself what you want more from a pet. If it's something cute and cuddly that would like to spend time on Colleen's lap, I'll find you something good."

"Well, she can't walk a dog very far yet, unless it's really well behaved. On the other hand, would a kitten hang around or take off?"

"Despite what some folks think, if you get a young kitten it can be trained to tolerate a collar, and even a leash. Not as easily with a dog, but cats are smart. When they realize they can't win, they give up."

Again she laughed, this time more comfortably. "So how long would that take?"

"I can probably do it for you in about a week."

She felt surprise. "You'd do that?"

"Of course. No charge. If Colleen really wants a kitten then I'd be glad to give her one that won't run off."

Del bit her lip. "It's just that I try to keep Colleen outside as much as possible when I'm making a lot of dust or using chemicals. I don't want her to suffer any harm. And I sure wouldn't want to bring an animal into an environment where it would have to be inside all the time with that stuff either."

"We're agreed then. Kitten or puppy?"

"Maybe I'm nuts, but if you think it's okay, I'd rather give her what she wants."

"I agree. Kitten it is. And I've got plenty over at the clinic. People drop them on my doorstep all the time. If you want, bring her over on Monday afternoon to pick one. Or let me work with a few for a week and find the one most amenable to a collar and leash."

Del thought about that. "I already know she wants a calico, so maybe surprising her would be more fun than making her wait for a week or so. Do you have any calicos?"

"Just one. They're relatively rare. But she's certainly a friendly little one. Loves to be hugged and petted."

"That sounds ideal then."

"Consider it done. But since it'll be me and one kitten *mano a mano,* rather than just picking the most cooperative animal, it might take a little longer to leash train it."

Again he had made her laugh, with the mental image of him in hand-to-hand combat with a stubborn kitten. "All right, I won't tell her."

"Probably best, unless you like to be nagged."

Her smile widened and she decided she liked Mike Windwalker. "I can't thank you enough."

"No thanks necessary. I'm always happy to find a good home for an animal."

"Well, I've kept you long enough." She started to turn away then saw her empty house waiting for her. And she stopped, unable to say why. Just that for some reason that house no longer looked as welcoming to her as it had when she bought it.

"This is ridiculous." Unaware she had spoken out loud, she was surprised when she heard a response.

"What is?" Mike asked.

She blew a long breath, impatient with herself, and now embarrassed. She should have made up some excuse, but she'd never been much of liar. "It's ridiculous that for some reason I don't want to go into that house tonight."

She was still staring at the building, but when she heard him move she looked at him. He stood straight up now, and he moved to her side, glancing at the house, too.

"I can't say," he said slowly, "that I don't understand what you're talking about."

Her heart slammed. What was he saying? Was he just trying to scare her? No, he didn't seem like the type. On the other hand, how well did she know him? "What do you mean?"

He gave a slight shake of his head, then shrugged. "Damned if I know." Slowly his dark-as-ebony eyes came to meet hers. "Want me to come in with you? Just to look around?"

She wanted to laugh the whole thing off, as if they were just joking, but somehow she couldn't. And as independent as she'd become since Don's death, she was surprised that his offer didn't put her hackles up.

Maybe because her hackles were already up over something she couldn't even define. "I must have eaten something that didn't agree with me," she said, trying to find a rational explanation for that lingering feeling of reluctance.

He didn't answer, just waited for her decision.

Finally, forcing briskness into her tone, she made it. "Sure, come on in and I'll show you around. Maybe you'll enjoy laughing at me."

"Why would I do that?"

"Because I was crazy enough to take on a project this size?"

At that he chuckled but shook his head. "I don't think you're crazy. I think you're a hard worker who isn't intimidated by huge jobs."

"Maybe I should have been intimidated with this one. Come on, I'll show you what I meant about the rot in the walls."

She thought he hesitated, but he was only a half step behind her as she led the way.

With each step she wondered what the heck was wrong with her. And why he could be so contrarily reluctant and friendly.

Walking into Del's house in plain sight of any nosy neighbor who might be watching through sheers or around the edges of curtains might not be the smartest act on the planet, Mike thought. On the other hand, he could sense how troubled Del felt, and he couldn't ignore that.

Just because some held on to old prejudices, it didn't mean everyone did. Hell, didn't this county have a couple of Native American lawmen?

But his people had been involved at Little Big Horn, something he'd had rubbed in his face for years when he was younger. Now that he was big enough to defend himself, most just plain didn't say anything, so he might well be attributing those animosities to more folks than deserved it.

But he knew damn well the prejudices were still there, whether in most or just a handful, and he hoped Del wouldn't suffer for what he was about to do. From what he could tell, she had quite enough problems on her plate.

Then he told himself to stop worrying about it. He was a grown-up and so was she. All that mattered was that she was nervous about entering her own house, and he'd learned early in life not to ignore those feelings. You might not be able to identify what triggered them, but ignoring them could get you into trouble.

As soon as he stepped through the front door, he looked around and remarked, "I can see why you bought this house."

She cocked an eye his way, smiling faintly. "Why?"

He waved one arm. "Most houses from this era are shotguns, one room behind another. But this one… Look at this wide hallway. And the stairway. In most places it would be right in the living room. It seems extravagant considering the era when it was built."

"It is." Her eyes brightened as she smiled. "I couldn't resist it because it's so different, and because it's more amenable to a modern lifestyle. When you have the shotgun floor plan, where rooms were just added straight back, it's hard to change things enough so that you're not walking through bedrooms. A real challenge. But this place is just perfect."

He lifted one eyebrow. "Except for all the hard work you have to do." That much was impossible to miss. Even the railing on the staircase had been painted, as had doors and moldings. He suspected there was plenty of fine wood to be uncovered in this house. "Somebody with money built this place."

"That's my guess, but I really haven't looked into the history of the house."

"You should. There's probably a fascinating story somewhere."

Yet, despite the architectural grace of the place, there they stood just inside the door. Mike hesitated, looking inward, trying to sense the cause for that. He'd gone through the house with her because she felt uneasy. Because something had made him feel a bit uneasy, too, yesterday, and again today. But instead of taking that walkthrough, they both stood here as if an invisible wall held them back.

His uneasiness had grown, he realized. But just a shade. Not enough to worry him. Finally, feeling the tension in the woman beside him, he asked, "Would you just like me to walk through on my own?"

He was willing, and a bit of a street fighter out of necessity. He could handle just about anyone who didn't have a gun. Although why the hell he should be worried about that he didn't know.

He paused a few seconds, searching places in himself that he usually kept hidden. There was something about this house...

Del gazed at him, her blue eyes reflecting perplexity and even some embarrassment. "What's going on?"

He got the feeling she was asking herself, not him. But he hesitated only a moment before saying, "This house feels sad."

She nodded, surprising him. "I never noticed anything before but..." She sighed. "Okay, I'm feeling really weird. I'm not an overly imaginative person. Maybe Colleen's complaint about noises is getting to me."

"Could be," he agreed smoothly, although for an instant he wanted to disagree strongly. But he'd turned himself into a man of science on purpose, and if he were to consider the empirical evidence, it was nuts to say the house felt sad. He managed a crooked smile. "I guess it must have gotten to me, too. Your daughter just doesn't seem like the kind of kid to think she has bears in her closet."

"She's not. We got past that stage before she turned four. So if she says she's hearing something, it's got to be mice in the walls."

"Or a water pipe ticking. I don't have to tell you how many sounds an old house can make."

"Plenty," she agreed. "And now I not only feel ridiculous, I feel stupid. You don't have to walk through with me. I'm sure you've got plenty to do."

He almost took it as a dismissal, which he was used to getting often enough in life. But her expression gave him pause. No, she hadn't lost her uneasiness, but she was feeling silly for it. He tried to think of a way to continue to accompany her while taking her concerns seriously. She was obviously a quite independent woman, and there was a good chance she didn't like leaning on a man, especially over an inexplicable feeling. And there was still something about this damn house.

"I'd actually like to see where Colleen's hearing the noises." He shrugged. "You never know. I might hear them and be able to identify them."

"I wish you could," she admitted. "I haven't heard them myself, at least not yet."

"So let's go hunting."

At that she chuckled and led the way.

The downstairs was quite spacious and nicely laid out. Kitchen and dining room on one side of the unusually large hallway, living room and an extra room on the other side. They skipped the extra room initially, though Mike could see color through the door that was slightly ajar.

Upstairs there were another three spacious bedrooms with walk-in closets and an unusually large bathroom that boasted an iron tub with clawed feet. A real antique, and a tub that a full-grown man could actually fit into.

"I wish this house had been available when I bought mine," he remarked. "I'd have snapped it up."

She flashed a smile. "You can always buy it once I get it fixed up."

"I may take you up on that."

The bedrooms, as yet, had clearly not been worked on, but even so their condition wasn't bad. Her room held an ordinary double bed and a dresser, and not one personal item was in view. He found that a little odd. The two others were empty.

When they returned downstairs, she led him to the room at the back end of the hall, the one they had skipped the first time through.

It proved to be Colleen's room and was a riot of color, with posters and a shiny mobile, and a bed nearly filled with pillows and stuffed animals. A lovely old table was obviously being used for a desk, high enough that the child's wheelchair could slide up to it comfortably, and it sported a good laptop computer along with books, papers and doodads. Over the bed was a bar hanging from a chain, probably to help Colleen maneuver into and out of her chair. He squashed a natural sympathetic reaction, because he sensed it would not be welcome either by Colleen or her mother. That child showed every sign of becoming just as independent as her mom.

"Does Colleen only hear the sounds in here?"

"So far. I've checked the attic and upstairs, but I haven't found any spoor, or anything else for that matter. I put in some traps but they haven't been sprung."

"Can we just stay here for a little bit?"

Del shrugged. "Sure. Why not?" She sat on the edge of the bed, leaving him to sit on a wooden chair in the corner, which meant moving an oversize stuffed rabbit.

"Does she only hear the sounds at night?"

"Mostly, but sometimes in the evening when she's in here doing homework. They've always stopped by the time I get in here when she calls me."

"That's…strange." Something warned him to be very careful here. There might be some emotional land mines he didn't want to trip by blundering around. "I like your daughter. She's so friendly for someone her age. I'm used to kids kind of glancing my way and dismissing me unless I'm caring for one of their pets."

"Kids that age are so awkward about things. Some of them anyway. Colleen has had so many adults in her life, in one capacity or another, since her accident that I think she's more comfortable with older people."

"That could be part of it. And she's certainly outgoing."

They sat a few minutes in silence and Mike realized that Del seemed to be growing uneasier, rather than less so. He wanted to ask what troubled her, but he didn't feel he knew her well enough.

"You know," Del said finally, "maybe I should sleep in here tonight. Colleen is spending the night with a friend, and it might be the perfect time to do a little more detective work."

He nodded. "Might be a good idea."

Suddenly her blue eyes, as sharp as lasers, met his. "Why did you say this house makes you feel sad?"

Crap. He'd kind of hoped she would let that go, because he never should have said it, even out of natural sympathy. "I don't know," he said finally. "It was just a feeling."

She nodded slowly. "I'm Irish enough to be superstitious. Or maybe I should say my mother raised me to be superstitious. Don't open an umbrella in the house, knock on wood, don't tempt fate, all those things. I rebelled against all of that, of course. Sometimes I even open an umbrella in the house just to prove I don't buy it."

Her lips curved almost impishly, and he had to smile back. "I hear you."

Her small smile faded. "But there's a definite atmosphere in this house I didn't notice before. I thought maybe I was imagining it because I couldn't find a source for the noises Colleen complains about. But then you said the house felt sad."

He wished he could take those words back. But he couldn't, and by saying them he'd not only revealed something about himself that he ordinarily kept private, but he'd apparently also increased Del's concern.

He ought to kick his own butt. "Sorry," he said. But he couldn't deny that he felt something in this house, because that would mean lying.

"It's okay. At least I know I'm not riding the crazy train alone." She sighed, then smiled. "Let me make us some coffee or something. We could probably sit here for hours and never hear the sound."

Long experience warned him to leave, that he'd been in her house long enough to stir talk if people had noticed. But another part of him, the real person who'd been tucked away inside out of necessity, told him to stick around. If she wanted him gone, she wouldn't have made the offer, and her suggestion that he stay intimated that she didn't want to be alone here. Nor could he blame her.

But she caught his hesitation, and he saw her fair cheeks color faintly. "I'm sorry," she said. "You just got home and I've already taken too much of your time."

This time he didn't hear a dismissal. Far from it: this was genuine courtesy. And it warmed him.

"I'd love that coffee if it's not too much trouble."

She hopped up from the bed, clearly pleased. "No trouble at all. In fact, I need to make dinner for myself, so why don't I just make it for both of us."

She hurried from the room, apparently intent on doing just that. He remained a moment longer, wondering if he'd just put his foot in it for both of them.

But the sadness in the house called to him, and he couldn't help thinking that, in her own way, Del was probably as lonely a soul as he was.

And that called to him, too.

In the big scheme of things, impulsively inviting a neighbor to stay for a cobbled-together dinner probably didn't amount to much. But for Del it was a big step. She liked to know her neighbors, yes, but rarely socialized beyond the most casual conversations. Not since the accident.

Once she'd been quite engaged with friends and a social life, but since Don's death she had begun to note how she had narrowed her world and limited the people she allowed to become close. In fact, she had even let close friends go, slowly, simply by not keeping up with them.

Afraid to make new connections because she was afraid of more pain? Yeah, and she knew it. But it didn't bother her. She had more than enough to occupy herself, and she could justify narrowing the scope of her life by the need to take care of Colleen.

So in the big scheme of things, asking Mike Windwalker to join her for dinner was nothing. In *her* scheme of things it seemed like a huge step. But, she assured herself as she began to pull things from the fridge and cupboards, it really was a minor thing. He'd offered to help her get an appropriate kitten for Colleen. Asking him to stay for a run-of-the-mill dinner hardly seemed out of line.

And maybe it was time for her to pull at least one foot out of her self-imposed rut. She wasn't opposed to healing—she just didn't seem to have time for it. Maybe she needed to make time, for the sakes of both her daughter and herself.

"What can I do to help?" Mike asked as he entered the kitchen.

"Have a seat and keep me company." She looked over her shoulder at him and said frankly, "I've turned myself into a hermit. It would be good for me to start practicing my social skills again."

He smiled as he pulled out a chair at the small table and sat. "I probably could use some of the same myself."

"I doubt it. You deal with people all day long. I deal with wood, plaster, paint and noxious chemicals. They don't talk back."

A chuckle escaped him. "You picked quite a profession."

"I enjoy it. I like working with my hands and solving the problems that go along with restoring a house."

He was silent a moment, then asked carefully, "Why'd you turn into a hermit?"

She faced him then, folding her arms and leaning back against the counter. "Truth or social quip?"

"I vastly prefer the truth to social ice skating."

At that she felt a smile tip up the corners of her mouth. A smile she hadn't expected. "Truth it is, then. My husband was killed in the accident that paralyzed Colleen. You know what they say about once burned, twice shy? I seem to have applied that lesson to everything except Colleen."

"I can definitely see how that might happen. I have a similar story, but I'll leave that for another time."

She could see his barriers snap into place, and her curiosity itched. But okay, she was willing to observe his boundaries. She expected the same courtesy for herself.

"Fair enough," she agreed and turned back to the counter. But she couldn't help wondering what his story was. "I hope you like salad."

"Any way it's made."

"Good." Because that was all she had planned tonight, a green salad with some leftover grilled chicken breast and a choice of bottled dressings. Her time was so limited these days that she stuck with basics, the quicker and easier the better, her only nod being to the healthfulness of what she prepared.

As she was standing at the counter slicing tomatoes, a bang sounded through the house.

She whirled around, her heart accelerating, and found Mike looking upward. "Door slamming," he said. "Do you have windows open or a fan on?"

"Not right now. I didn't open anything when I came home."

He rose. "Stay here. I'll go look."

"Like hell," she answered. She'd been using her chef's knife to slice, and she seated it more firmly in her grip. A weapon.

He didn't argue with her as she followed him. For that she gave him points.

"Sounded like it was from upstairs," he remarked quietly.

"It did," she agreed. In the hallway it was easy to see at a glance that all the doors stood wide open, the way they'd been left. Mike glanced at her, acknowledging that he'd noticed, too.

And then he started up the stairs, stepping to the outside of the risers so as not to make noise. She followed his example.

But at the top of the stairs, they could see all the doors were open, just as they'd been left.

He spoke. "Could something in the attic have made that sound?"

"There's nothing up there. Not so much as a box."

They both stood for a minute, listening, but no other sound disturbed the utter silence of the house.

"It must have come from outside." But even as Del spoke the dismissal, she knew she was lying to herself. That noise had come from inside, not from without. And there was no mistaking the sound of one of these solid oak doors slamming.

"Well," said Mike slowly, apparently agreeing with

her thought if not her words, "if one of those doors slammed open it would have been hard enough to leave some evidence."

Del watched as he checked in every room. She didn't need to look for herself because she knew exactly what the sound was, and it wasn't a door opening. As often as she had the windows open and fans going, she absolutely knew how these doors sounded when they slammed shut, and it wasn't the same as when they got caught on a gust and were pushed open. Not the same at all.

Mike returned in only a few moments. "Let me check the attic," he said.

She looked at him, realizing he wasn't criticizing her, understanding that he was genuinely concerned someone other than the two of them might be inside the house. Heck, the back of her *own* neck was prickling with that suspicion.

But surely if someone were in the house, they would have discovered it on their walk-through. Unless, as Mike apparently feared, someone was in the attic.

God, the idea made her skin crawl. She waited with forced patience as Mike pulled down the overhead ladder to the attic and climbed up. She heard him flip the switch which turned on three bulbs that hung from the rafters from one end of the attic to another. He reappeared only a minute later.

"Nobody could hide up there unless they're six inches tall."

"I know." And somehow that only made this worse.

Noises for no reason? She'd lived in this house for over two months now, and she knew its sounds as intimately as she knew her own heartbeat. That had been the sound of an oak door slamming. Hard. And in the usual way, they wouldn't do that even with the windows open and the fans blowing, even with a relatively strong breeze in the house.

Inevitably, she thought about the sounds Colleen had been hearing and tried to put it together. But it made no sense.

Mike closed the attic trapdoor and looked at her, his gaze trailing down to the knife she held. "Loaded for bear?" he asked lightly.

A faint flush stung her cheeks. "Stupid, huh?"

He shook his head. "I was just thinking that you look like you could take on the whole damn world. That's a compliment."

"Thanks." But now she felt foolish. She'd investigated odd sounds many times in her life, but never before had she felt compelled to carry a knife on the hunt. "Major overreaction."

"Not really. Not when you consider that Colleen has been complaining of noises. That'd raise *my* action-alert level, too."

He really *was* a very nice man. Her embarrassment seeped away and she turned for the stairs. "Let's go get that salad."

He also turned out to be a comfortable companion. She felt no pressure to talk as she finished the salad and served them at the table. She often spent large chunks of her time inside her own head, busy with her hands, and most of the time she preferred it that way. There was a soothing rhythm in her work, and it left her feeling content at day's end.

Someone who could share that silence while seeming to remain comfortable was unusual indeed.

"I don't spend much time on cooking," she said

apologetically as she put the last bottle of dressing on the table. "Healthy foods are the best I can do, as quickly as possible. Oh! I have some frozen garlic bread, if you'd like some."

"This is fine." He smiled and gestured her to sit with him. "I don't cook much at all myself. A fresh salad is a treat."

She returned his smile and motioned him to serve himself first. "With Colleen I probably keep a better eye on things than I would otherwise."

"Understandable. I think the animals in my kennel have a far better diet than I do. When I get sick of bottles, cans and frozen foods, I go to Maude's."

"Maude's is one of my guilty pleasures, too. I'm surprised I haven't seen you there."

"I don't go often." Something in his tone suggested there was a reason for that, and she wondered but didn't say anything. She didn't know him well enough to ask any personal questions.

She paused just as she poked her fork into a bit of tomato, as the sound of the slamming door sounded once again, this time in her head. "I'm sorry," she said after a moment. "I don't think I can hold a normal conversation right now."

He put his own fork down and looked attentively at her. "The noise we heard?"

"That and the noises Colleen is hearing. Yesterday I was wondering if she was imagining them, and not knowing what was worse—her imagining them or the sounds being real when I couldn't find the source." She tightened her lips. "I didn't imagine that slam."

"Hardly. I heard it, too, remember?"

She hesitated, then said, "Colleen has been through

hell. So much so that I keep waiting for her to shatter in some way. I mean, to lose your dad and be paralyzed all at once, at her age…" She trailed off as her throat tightened. Finally she found her voice gain. "Except for the first month or so, she's been an amazing trouper."

"I get that impression. So you were wondering if her hearing things was the shattering you feared?"

"It crossed my mind. Awful of me even to think that."

"No, I think it was reasonable to wonder. Look, I doctor animals, but I've seen them with post-traumatic stress reactions, too. With some of them, they seem fine at first, and then one day they start acting out somehow. Your fear was entirely reasonable. But apparently that's not what's going on."

"Apparently not. And now I've got to wonder what caused that sound. Maybe we misinterpreted something else."

"That's possible." He pushed back from the table. "Tell you what. I'm going to go through the house and slam doors. You holler out when you hear the one that sounds like what we heard."

She nearly gaped at him, then felt almost embarrassed, though she wasn't sure why. "I think I invited you to join me for dinner. You should finish eating first."

A soft chuckle escaped him. "Salad will keep for five minutes, and I'm as curious as you are. Let me go slam some doors. You sing out if one of them sounds the same."

In the doorway, he paused to look back. "Stand where you were before, if you don't mind. That way we can be sure it was the same sound."

"Okay." She was actually glad to hop up and go stand

by the counter, facing the same direction. She *needed* to solve this problem, the sooner the better. Then maybe she could put Colleen's fears to rest and silence her own concerns.

Maybe.

She stood leaning against the counter, eyes closed, listening to slam after slam, first from downstairs, then from upstairs. The bangs moved through the house, but by the time Mike returned she was certain of one thing.

"None of them, huh?" he asked as he returned to the kitchen.

She pivoted to face him. "The sound was similar on the upstairs doors. But I noticed something else."

"What?"

"The vibration passed through the whole house when you slammed them."

His eyes widened a hair. "So we heard the sound, but there was no vibration. You're right. I didn't *feel* the door slam."

"Nope." And what had been a small worry blossomed into a big fear.

"This is not good," he said.

She couldn't have agreed more.

Chapter 3

"I don't believe in hauntings," she said as they washed up after the meal. Hunger had pretty much deserted them, and there was a lot of salad left. And haunting was the only other explanation her mind kept turning up for the sound of a door slamming when none had.

"No?" His question was neutral.

She looked at him as she handed him the last plate to dry and realized he wasn't looking at her. "Do you?"

"I was raised in a different culture."

She reached for a spare towel and dried her hands. "I'd like to hear about that if you don't mind telling me."

He shrugged one shoulder and put the dried plate in the cupboard with the rest. "I'm a man of science. I'm supposed to believe in the mechanistic view of life."

"But you don't?"

"Only insofar as it's useful."

Curious, she grabbed a couple of fresh coffee cups and filled them, putting them on the table before he could refuse and thus insist it was time to leave. She was well aware that she was taking a lot of his time, but she wasn't ready to let him go. Couldn't, if she were to be honest about it. Sitting in this house alone wondering about that noise was apt to keep her up all night.

He hesitated but didn't argue. She made up her mind right then that one of these days she was going to get to the root of the way he hesitated about so many things. But not now. She had just asked enough of him for one night.

"I'm sorry I can't offer you a more comfortable place to sit."

One corner of his mouth lifted. "I'm a table-and-chair kind of person. My family held every gathering around a table."

"Mine, too." At least a point of connection.

As soon as she returned to her seat at the table, he joined her. "So what did you mean?" she prodded gently.

"I'm Cheyenne. I know, dirty word around here."

"Not in this house," she informed him firmly.

Again that half smile of his. "How'd you avoid it?"

"I was always weird."

This time a real laugh escaped him. "Weird how?"

"Well, I got into a bit of trouble when I was six. I was in religious education class and when the teacher said Judas went to hell for betraying Christ, I asked how that could be possible, since God had planned it all and *somebody* had to do it."

"Wow. How much trouble did you get into?"

"Only a little, actually. But that was my first starring

role as the girl who asks off-the-wall questions." She shook her head a bit. "My dad took me to the memorial of the Battle of Little Big Horn when I was about fourteen, and all I could think was that Custer was an idiot."

That, too, surprised a laugh out of him. "How did your dad react to that?"

"He surprised me by saying it did look that way. When I got older I learned a word for Custer's idiocy—*hubris*. The man was full of it. I mean, even ignoring that we were busy taking all the land away from you folks, and hunting you down like animals, Custer was an idiot. When I stood where the cavalry stood, and looked down that hill at where all the Cheyenne—I seem to remember it was mostly Cheyenne along with some other Sioux tribes—all I could think is what idiot with two hundred and forty-five soldiers attacks five thousand people?"

"The battle began long before that day."

"I know." She sighed. "It's a sad and ugly story. And all the folks in these parts who talk as if you guys are still the enemy would be feeling a whole lot different if they'd been invaded. So no, we don't share those feelings in this house. Memories are too damned long anyway."

"Even among my people."

"With more reason."

"That's debatable, too."

She noticed he seemed to have relaxed, really relaxed for the first time since crossing her threshold. Well, considering the ill-considered bigotry a lot of people spouted, she could understand that. "So about how you were raised?"

"Many Native American people believe that all things are sentient, even the rocks. And many of us believe the spirit world exists right alongside us. And sometimes we get glimpses of that world."

She bit her lip. "So you believe in hauntings?"

"Honestly? I'm not sure. I'm just not ready to dismiss anything out of hand. But I'm definitely willing to help you keep looking for the source of that sound. Because however I was raised, I'd still like to find a concrete explanation."

She guessed she could deal with that. When she thought about it, what he was saying was really no different from what her religion taught: there was a spirit world, and afterlife. She just didn't believe the two intersected. "So you're not trying to tell me the house is haunted."

"I'd hardly jump to that conclusion from a single sound."

She sipped her coffee and regarded him thoughtfully. "You must feel sometimes as if you walk in two worlds."

"Sometimes."

She tried to read something in his expression, but this man gave away little he didn't choose to. Still, she could imagine that straddling two different cultures probably carried difficulties she couldn't begin to understand. And then there was bigotry. She'd heard enough talk in these parts to know that was still alive and well among some when it came to Native Americans.

"You probably could have chosen any place in the country to practice," she said after a few moments. "Why did you come here?"

"Because it was near enough that I could get home

to see my mother. At the time, she wasn't in the best of health."

"I'm sorry."

"That's life, isn't it?"

"Unfortunately, yes." She sighed and lifted her coffee mug in both hands. "I grew up here, but I almost didn't come back."

"No?"

"I met Don, my husband, in college, and he got a job in Denver. I followed after I graduated." She smiled faintly. "I'd studied architectural engineering and was lucky enough to land a job with a firm in Denver. So we married, and Colleen came along, and the world was my oyster. Our oyster. After the accident, after Colleen recovered enough to need physical therapy only a few times a week, I realized I couldn't bear to stay there any longer. It felt as if there was a reminder around every corner. So I ran back home."

His nod was encouraging, his expression sympathetic. "Has it turned out well?"

"I've been able to move on, if that's what you mean. I'm busy, I feel good most days about most things. Unfortunately, I studied architectural engineering and these days I wished I'd stayed longer and taking mechanical engineering, too. You know, wiring and plumbing. I have to hire people to do that work."

"Expensive?"

"Of course." She gave a rueful shrug. "The minute I start tearing out walls and putting in bathrooms, I have to bring everything up to code. And while I approve of building codes, it would be nice if I could do that work myself."

"I suppose going back for training would be difficult now."

"Now, yes. Maybe later on." She sipped more coffee and looked at him over the mug. "What made you decide to become a veterinarian?"

"Animals." His smile was beautiful. "From the time I was little I loved animals. They didn't always get treated very well on the rez because we were poor. Lots of strays. You know, that was an odd contrast. Spiritually we think of animals as our brothers. But in reality…" He shrugged a shoulder. "When you're having trouble feeding a kid, it's hard to find food for a dog. So there were a lot of strays. Mostly dogs, some cats, but cats actually do better for themselves on their own. I started collecting them, much to my mother's chagrin. And I found a low-paying job when I was eight, watching a neighbor's sheep, and used the money to buy dog food. I put my first splint on a dog's leg when I was ten because nobody could afford to take a stray to a vet and the only other alternative was to shoot it."

"Did the splint work?"

"You bet. Mainly because I was lucky and it was a simple fracture." He chuckled quietly. "But there was no stopping me after that. I learned a lot about caring for livestock from my elders. I read books. I scoured libraries and finally got really lucky."

"How so?"

"A vet who came to the rez sometimes to look after cattle and sheep picked up on my interest and took me on as an assistant."

"That's great!" But she saw his face shadow and realized the unhappiness inherent in that story, as well as the pleasure of having an opportunity. A complex man, one who kept a lot close to the vest.

"Yes, it was. He gave me a load of books to read, he taught me, and he made sure I studied hard enough and well enough to get into college. A good man."

"He sounds like it."

"I was lucky to have a mentor, a great mentor. People like that can make more of a difference than they may ever realize. Unfortunately, he died before I graduated from veterinary school, but at least he knew I made it."

"I'm sure he was proud."

"Despite everything."

She opened her mouth to ask what he meant, but she realized his face had closed as suddenly as someone slamming a door. She bit back the words and sat there, feeling at sea, wondering if there was any direction with this man that didn't lead to a closed door, or a hesitation, or the sense there was a lot he would never say.

Of course, that just made her even more curious, but she knew how to bide her time. She'd learned patience the hard way, with a daughter whose slow recovery demanded it.

A rumble of thunder drew her attention and she glanced toward the kitchen window, surprised to see the light had begun to turn a gray-green.

"That'll upset the dogs in the kennel," Mike remarked.

"Really?"

"About thirty percent of dogs are scared of storms. In a kennel, that thirty percent set off the rest."

"Is it the noise?"

"There's some debate about that. Some dogs seem to

start responding way too early, as if they sense a change in the air pressure."

"Amazing. Do you need to go to them?"

"No, that only reinforces the behavior. We all, me included, wish there was some way to comfort them, but there isn't. They interpret the comfort as positive reinforcement, and it makes it worse. And right now we don't have any dogs who freak out enough to require sedation. So the best thing to do is let it burn itself out."

"That must be hard to do."

"It is, I admit. I have to remind myself often enough that trying to soothe them will make it harder on them in the long run." He gave a faint smile. "When it comes to animals, I'm a natural-born hugger."

She returned his smile. "That's a good thing. I like people who want to hug kids and animals. It's the ones who don't that concern me. So you can really leash-train a cat? I'm still trying to imagine that."

"Oh, Colleen won't be able to walk her, or anything like that. But she can be trained to accept leash limitations. By that I mean if she's sitting on Colleen's lap and decides she wants to run after a bird, she won't throw a clawing, hissy cat fit because she can't get any farther than six feet. She may glare her disapproval, but before long she'll climb back on Colleen's lap, and eventually she'll stop trying to run after things outside."

"I was raised with the notion that you can't teach cats anything."

He laughed quietly. "Cats do a good job of keeping it a secret. I had my last cat perfectly trained. I fed him when he wanted, played when he wanted, and…he never

ever tried to get out the door after just a few attempts when I caught him and dragged him back in. He learned his limits. The same way he learned to stay out of the fridge when the door accidentally shut on him, catching him in the side."

"Oh, my!"

"*That* only took one lesson." His dark eyes danced. "One of the main differences between cats and dogs is that dogs are eager to please. More of a pack mentality. Cats…well, less so."

Thunder rumbled again, this time louder. This time Mike glanced at the window, and Del noticed that the kitchen was definitely darker now.

He looked at her. "Are you going to be okay by yourself tonight?"

"Because of the noise, you mean? Of course I will. It's just a noise. With my luck I'll probably find out another wall stud just collapsed or something. I'll be honest. I knew there was some rot in the place, but I didn't expect it to be quite so extensive. And then down in the basement there's this ridiculous brick wall that's starting to crumble a bit."

"A brick wall?"

"I know. Weird. I guess someone thought it would be attractive, like they started refinishing the basement and never got around to completing the job. But it's just dark. The thing is, I keep wondering if, when I tear it out, I'm just going to find that there's a big gaping hole in the concrete. That's the way everything else in this house is going." She gave a little shake of her head and a rueful smile. "At least the roof is solid."

"Maybe you just need to bulldoze underneath."

She laughed, imagining propping up the roof while

destroying the house beneath it. "Don't tempt me. But actually, there's a positive side to all this."

"Tell me."

"I get to remake most of the place. The load-bearing walls so far seem to be fine, but since so much else is a mess, I can reconfigure the floor plan in lots of ways I wouldn't have attempted otherwise. A work-through rather than a work-around." She stared past him for a few seconds, envisioning it. "This may become the house I stay in. If I'm going to do all this work, I may as well enjoy the fruits."

"What would you do differently if you decide to stay, as opposed to just selling it?"

"I'd make the kitchen more accessible to Colleen. And I'd do a complete finish-out of the bath off her bedroom so it would be perfect for her."

"Then do it."

She looked at him, surprised by his encouragement. "I've been seriously thinking about it."

He hesitated just a moment then asked, "Is she always going to be in that chair?"

"Barring a medical miracle."

"Then fix the place for her."

She gave him a rueful look. "Only if I can find the source of the sounds that are scaring her."

"True. How scared is she?"

"Scared enough. At first when I said it must be vermin in the walls or the attic, she seemed okay with it. But as time passes and I don't find anything, I can tell it's starting to frighten her."

He nodded. "This calls for some thinking, then. I'll put my mind to it and see what I can come up with." He rose from the table and rinsed his coffee cup at the sink before tucking it into the new dishwasher. "Thanks for everything. If I come up with any ideas, I'll let you know."

She saw him out and closed the door behind him, catching glimpses of him through the front window as he walked back over to his house.

A nice guy, certainly concerned about Colleen. But at the same time, she felt he hadn't been quite comfortable his whole time here.

She let out a heavy sigh and wondered if she was imagining things herself. Why should he be uncomfortable? No reason that she could see. And he'd certainly tried to be helpful.

The thunder rumbled again, like an approaching beast, and she realized she was standing all alone in a darkening house where even she, now, had heard an inexplicable noise.

For an instant she had that horrible feeling, the one most people referred to as *something just walked over my grave*.

Not good. As a single mom with a child, she couldn't let her imagination run away with her.

Not even when she was alone.

She slept in Colleen's bed that night, determined to hear whatever it was that Colleen was hearing. Or at least she tried to sleep. She kept waking from dreams that involved Mike Windwalker, and every one of them seemed to be sexy.

Man, she didn't need that. She'd buried that part of herself ever since the accident, first out of grief, and then out of the necessity of caring for her daughter and building some kind of hopeful life for them.

Yes, he was a sexy man. Yes, he was eye candy. But that didn't give him the right to turn up in her dreams, talking in that calm, deep voice of his, looking at her from dark eyes that seemed to be lit with some kind of inner flame. Nor did it give her sleeping brain the right to conjure images of him touching her, undressing her, kissing her…and waking her in a state of aching arousal.

Darn it!

Finally, sick of waking in tangled sheets, sick of waking to overwhelming need for a man's loving, she kicked her way out from under the covers and sat up.

Last night's storm still rumbled, though more quietly, and the rain seemed to have stopped. If not, it was falling so quietly she couldn't hear it through the closed windows.

The room felt chilly, but that didn't surprise her. It was still spring, nights cooled down fast and she didn't have the heat on.

Not even during her teens had she experienced these kinds of dreams. What was she doing having them at the advanced age of thirty-four? Shouldn't her hormones have quieted some?

Thunder growled again in the distance and a flash of faraway lightning brightened the room just a bit. She loved thunderstorms, and if all sleeping was going to give her was a taste of unrestrained libido, then there was no point in even trying.

Feeling grumpy—hardly surprising, she supposed—she shoved her feet into the sandals she'd kicked off before lying down in a T-shirt and shorts. When she was at this point of renovation, slippers weren't allowed, only hard-soled shoes. You never knew where a nail or splinter might turn up.

Rising, she smoothed the covers on Colleen's bed then turned to go get a drink and something to read. Maybe she could fall asleep on the sofa.

That was when she heard it.

A not very loud sound, but definitely a scratching, like fingernails on something rough.

She froze, straining her ears, and was rewarded with another rumble of thunder, one that now irritated her even more. Slowly it trailed away, as if reluctant to give up its voice, and silence reigned.

Again she heard the scratching. Faint. Weak. Impossible to say where it came from. Impossible to even be sure it came from within the room, it was so soft.

But she understood now why it disturbed Colleen so. It most definitely didn't sound like a mouse scrambling through the wall.

No, it sounded like something that wanted to get out. Something that wasn't strong enough. It was, she thought crazily, an almost plaintive sound.

And that was enough to make the hair on the back of her neck stand on end.

Chapter 4

Something woke Mike. He wasn't sure exactly what it was, but it brought him bolt upright in bed, not at all usual for him.

And the instant he awoke, he knew something was wrong. Not for one second did he question the instinct. A childhood spent at the knee of his uncle, a respected medicine man, had given him lessons no amount of time among science and Europeans could erase. Sometimes there was a *knowing*. Sometimes dreams whispered a truth, or the thunder spoke a message, or even the very molecules of the air carried a warning. He didn't need to know its source to listen to it.

Rising, he stepped into his jeans and pulled on a sweatshirt. Then he jammed his feet into the moccasins he wore around the house as slippers and began to move.

He let himself be guided, though he had no idea where he was going or why.

He *was* surprised, though, to be guided onto his front porch. The thundery night shimmered with distant lightning, nothing close enough to worry about. But in one of those flashes he saw a figure standing on Del's front porch. He tensed immediately, then in another shimmer saw that it was Del herself standing out there.

Immediately galvanized, he jumped over his porch railing and trotted her way, forgetting everything life had ever taught him about getting involved with a white woman.

"Del? Del?"

She turned as she heard his call. In the uneven, flickering light her expression was hard to read. He trotted up her steps and went to her side. "What's wrong?"

Her eyes looked like two dark holes until the lightning flashed again and he could see how wide and blue they were.

"I heard it," she said.

"The door slam?"

"No. The sounds Colleen is complaining about."

"You couldn't localize it?"

"I couldn't *stand* it."

He stilled, unsure what she meant, but troubled by the way she said it. He wanted to offer her that culture-crossing gesture of support, an arm around her shoulders, to ease her distress, but he knew better. Even if she claimed not to be a bigot, life had taught him that even that could change in the crunch. After all, Livvie's foot had kicked him, too, when he was down. Livvie's voice had cried the same insults. He understood why, and he had forgiven her eventually, but he'd learned his lesson.

Finally he asked, "Why couldn't you stand it?"

"Because… Oh, God, this is going to sound insane."

"I'm the only one listening, and I don't make that judgment. Out of my field."

She wrapped her arms around herself, shook her head once, then said, "Oh, hell, why not? If I'm crazy I need to know it."

"What exactly did you hear?"

"Scratching. But not like a mouse or a rat would do. It didn't sound like that. And I didn't hear anything moving. Nothing at all. It was just this very weak *scratching*. But…" She bit off the word and shook her head again.

"But what?"

She bit her lip, fighting with herself, he guessed. Then, "Honestly, Mike, it sounded like something was trying to scratch its way out of something. But as if it was too weak to do it. I swear it sounded almost like it was begging. And that's *nuts*."

Her gaze returned to his, vanishing and reappearing in the flicker of the distant lightning. For a second or two, he just absorbed her words, trying to add up her statements. When he did, he understood her discomfort.

He turned and looked at the house. Slowly he said, "I told you the place feels sad."

"What the hell does that mean?"

"I don't know." He looked at her, drawing back emotionally, prepared for the worst. But the worst didn't happen. Her expression was pleading, not accusatory.

"I'm going in," he said. "Colleen's bedroom?"

She nodded.

"I'll sit in there and listen."

"I'll come, too."

"No." He reached out and made the mistake of touching her forearm. Skin as smooth as satin, and the shock of the contact headed straight for his groin. Not now. Not her. No way.

"Just wait here," he said as he jerked his hand back. "Two people will make too much noise."

She nodded slowly, accepting his reasoning. He didn't tell her he was going to listen with more than his ears. Those were things you seldom shared with whites. At least in these parts.

He slipped through the open front door, his moccasins silent on bare wood and rugs both. He knew his way now and needed no more illumination than the occasional flash of the storm.

You feel so sad, he thought to the house. *What's your story? What happened?*

But there was no answer, and he didn't really expect one. The spirits seldom bothered to speak or explain, but his grandfather had taught him to respect them, to acknowledge them always. They were, after all, as much a part of this world as he was, seen or unseen.

In Colleen's room, he sat on her desk chair, closed his eyes and waited patiently. The rumbling of thunder in the distance was a familiar voice to him, one he had been taught to always listen to, not so much with his mind, but with his heart.

And his heart kept saying that something was wrong, very wrong, in this house.

His people believed in the sentience of everything in

the universe. Even the rocks, the water, the very air were aware. That storm in the distance was a living thing.

This house was aware. Not necessarily in the way of a human, but it was aware, and something made it sad. It had a story it could not tell, but it pierced his heart.

And maybe, just maybe, it wasn't only the house, for he could almost feel another whisper through that part of him that had been taught to listen for voices other than the human.

He sighed, trying to open himself even more, the scientifically trained portion of his brain fighting to get in the way of older teachings. If anyone around here ever heard him talk this way, he'd be out of work in a flash.

But he could not bury or deny the lessons of his youth. Nor could he quite open himself with the freedom he had known as a child, before life had gotten complicated with other philosophies, other thoughts, other beliefs.

Funny how he could go to the school on the rez, go to Mass in the mornings and hear of God, and saints and angels, and most of the folks around here held to similar notions, but if he mentioned that his own beliefs went one step farther…well. Had not the Creator created everything out of himself? Because what other materials could the Creator have used?

At least the teachers at his school had respected his tribal beliefs. Previous generations of his people had not fared so well in that regard, which until a few decades ago had driven the medicine men, like his uncle, virtually underground.

But his upbringing had benefited from more open minds, and he had managed a cultural and spiritual blending that didn't feel oppositional, that fit with reasonable comfort in his heart and mind. Not that these ideas would be welcomed around here.

His thoughts continued to meander because it was virtually impossible to silence them. Even as he tried to listen with his "other ears" to the voices that regular ears couldn't detect, his mind refused to settle.

Then he heard the scratching sound. He stiffened and waited, trying to determine where the sound came from. When he heard it again, it seemed to come from elsewhere. Weak. Distant.

Dying.

He waited longer, while the sadness of the house pressed in on him like a heavy weight, and then realized he would not hear it again. Some internal sense said whatever it might be, it had finished for the night.

He rose and went out to the front porch where Del waited. She looked cold, and he immediately felt guilty for taking so long.

"I heard it," he said.

"So I'm not losing my mind?"

"Absolutely not. I'm sorry, you're freezing out here."

She shook her head. "I could have gone in. I just didn't want to. Any idea what it is?"

"None. I thought I might recognize it, but I didn't."

"Well, okay, then. At least I know it's *something*. Colleen heard it, I heard it and now you heard it. Nobody is going crazy. So now I just have to figure out what it is."

"And we need to get you warmed up." He hesitated just briefly, too briefly for her to notice, he hoped. "You want to come over to my place? I at least have my heat on."

"Yeah." She gave a small, mirthless laugh. "One of my economies, keeping the heat off at night when it's not going to get that cold."

"Well, like I said, mine's on. Up to you. I can make us some coffee or some instant hot chocolate while you decide what you want to do about this."

She nodded then looked down at herself. "I'm not exactly dressed for a social call."

Which, of course, caused him to notice how little she wore: a T-shirt and shorts, and since her nipples had hardened prominently, he knew she wore no bra. Sexy beyond belief. He had to drag his gaze back to her face. It wasn't easy, considering the sight had caused an instant, unexpected pulse of need to head straight for his groin. In the blink of an eye, he grew hot and heavy.

He didn't need this. At all. "Want me to run in and find you something?"

She looked from him to the house. "I'm no wimp. But something about that sound seriously disturbed me."

"Me, too. Well, just come over to my place then."

She arched a rueful brow at him, barely visible in the night. "I need to lock up. I have too many expensive tools and supplies in there. And my keys are in my purse. In the house." She sighed. "This is ridiculous. I'm letting a sound drive me out of my own house."

"Most things are more unnerving at night. And more so if you're alone."

"True."

"I'll come in with you. We'll get your purse and at least a jacket."

She looked his way again. "Thanks. I keep telling myself to tough it out."

"How about you tough it out in daylight?" Then he

made an offer that must have surely risen from some unconscious part of his brain, because he knew better. "I'll help you look for a cause in the morning, if you want."

"That's a very kind offer. Okay, I'll get some sweats and my purse, and then I'll take you up on that hot chocolate."

He followed her back into the house and waited at the foot of the stairs while she ran up to get some clothes. At least the sense of oppression had lifted, gone as if it had never been, leaving him to wonder if somehow his imagination had run amok and had created the whole impression out of nothing.

Judging by the speed with which Del returned wearing a sweat suit, however, he suspected she didn't feel the same lifting of the atmosphere. Or was past caring.

Thunder still rumbled in the east, louder now as if the storm was growing. Lightning which had just a short while ago merely seemed to illuminate the clouds could now be seen forking down in brilliant bolts.

After Del locked the front door, they hurried across the yard and the driveway and into his house. In the moments just before they climbed his steps, he watched a brilliant fork of lightning shoot down, and it almost seemed to him to outline a woman's profile.

The voice of the storm? Imagination? Merely his brain constructing something familiar from lines, as brains were wont to do? Sometimes straddling worlds was a bitch.

The thought brought a faint smile of amusement to his lips as he opened his door for Del. An awkward time to feel amusement, but this was just plain an awkward time anyway. Here he was, doing what he'd vowed never to do again: get involved with a white woman.

The universe had a wicked sense of humor.

Inside he turned on enough lights to make her feel comfortable, then settled her in his living room. One of those rooms he had furnished straight out of a store, as inexpensively as he could, because he simply didn't have the patience to do anything else, or the desire to waste time. It was comfortable enough for his needs, and he supposed the fact that all the pieces matched might mean something to someone. For himself, he didn't much care.

The cocoa was instant, requiring nothing more than heating the water and adding a dollop of half-and-half for richness. He carried the mugs back to the living room and found Del curled up tightly on herself on one end of the couch.

"Feeling that bad?" he asked as he passed her a mug. She accepted it with both hands.

"No. Not exactly. I'm still a little cold. And I'm angry."

"Angry why?" He took an upholstered chair facing her.

"Because this is scaring Colleen. Because it scared me and I know better."

"Better than what?"

She arched her brow at him. "It's got to be an animal in the wall. What else could it be?"

He didn't answer, mainly because he was pretty sure she wouldn't like the kind of answer his uncle would have given her, and that was the only thing that would spring to his mind right now.

"Yeah, it sounded weird," she went on. "Strange. But

who knows what kind of effect all that lath and plaster has on sounds from inside the walls? I've never had it happen before, so how would I recognize the sound? I usually renovate one room at a time, but maybe this time I just ought to go through the whole place and strip all the walls down to the lath. If there's something there, it'll show up or leave."

"True." As long as it was an animal.

She sipped her cocoa. "This is good."

"Just instant."

"More than instant. I know, I make instant all the time."

"Well, I probably just hardened your arteries by adding some cream."

At that a faint smile curved her lips. "That's okay. Once never killed anybody unless jumping off tall buildings."

He admired the way she found humor, even when she was obviously stressed. "Tell me about Colleen," he said. "She impresses me every time I see her."

"She's an impressive kid. I honestly wouldn't have expected her to handle this mess so well."

"You mean being confined to a chair?"

"That and losing her dad at the same time. But yes, I guess most especially that." She sighed, sipped more cocoa and then unfolded enough to put her cup on a coaster on the end table. "Getting over her dad's death seemed to be the hardest part for her. Sometimes she still mentions how much she misses him."

"What happened?"

"Car accident. They'd gone together for a day of skiing. I had to stay home to work on a rush project. Anyway, on the way back it turned really cold and the wet pavement started to ice over. A car zipped around them as they were descending from the Eisenhower Tunnel, skidded and spun out. Don didn't have a chance to avoid it."

"I'm sorry." Inadequate words, but all words were.

"One of those things." She sighed, looking sad for a few moments. "You know, when you said my house feels sad, maybe it's me you're picking up on."

He started to shake his head, then let it lie. This was not the time to tell her the truth. "You and Colleen actually seem to have adjusted very well."

"Yeah. And sometimes it worries me. I keep waiting for Colleen to crash. She seems to have adjusted too well, if you know what I mean."

"It may happen from time to time," he agreed. "But some of us are born to be more philosophical about things than others. Some people just take it on the chin and move on with a smile. I've known a few."

"Are you one?"

"Unfortunately, no." He felt a rueful smile form on his lips. "I'm more the once-burned-twice-shy kind."

She nodded, and a soft smile eased her own expression a bit. "Most people are, I think. I know I am. Maybe I'm being ridiculous, but with Colleen I keep waiting for the other shoe to drop, if you know what I mean. Bad things happen. And when they happen to you, you no longer feel immune. So when she started hearing these noises, I actually—I think I told you this? I can't remember—I actually started wondering about her mental state, if things might finally be catching up with her."

"Apparently you don't need to worry about that anymore."

"Apparently not. And that's a great relief, from that

perspective. But now I know why the sound unnerves her so much, and I've *got* to get to the root of it. *I* heard it and had to get out of that house."

"I'll help you every way I can." He mentally kicked his own butt as soon as the words were out, but his nature required no less than that he help. And leaving her to deal with it alone—which he was sure she would do because trying to explain it to someone who hadn't heard the sounds would be impossible—went against everything he believed about community. "I'll help," he said again. "I may not know much about renovation, but I'm sure I can rip out walls."

That garnered a sigh from her, and she seemed to relax a bit. "That's the fun part. But if I'm going to do all that, I'll need to ask my aunt to take care of Colleen."

"You sound reluctant."

"Well, she's getting up there. Physically she couldn't do much to help if Colleen needed to be lifted."

"How far away does she live? Because she and Colleen could stay here in my house until we clear out enough of the mess."

Her eyes widened, and for an instant he almost thought tears moistened her eyes. "You're a very kind man, Mike Windwalker."

Yeah, right. And it was a damn good thing he had his legs crossed so she couldn't see the more selfish feelings on parade.

He let her comment pass because he really couldn't answer it.

Any way he looked at it, dawn couldn't arrive quick enough.

Curled up on Mike Windwalker's couch, Del felt more comfortable than she had in days, maybe since Colleen had started complaining about the noises in her room. They would get started at dawn, and she wasn't going to stop until she found the sources of those noises. For now she was out of the house, unable to worry needlessly until she could act, and Mike had made her feel that she wasn't alone.

Not that anyone was truly alone in Conard County. Neighbors were always quick to help, but they had to know you needed help, and it had to be something they could actually do. So far she hadn't told anyone but Mike about the noises, mainly because she feared for Colleen's mental state.

But now Mike had heard the noises, too, so she could rest about Colleen, and she would even have help getting at the root of the problem.

Having heard the sounds that plagued Colleen, she was more disturbed than before. When she'd been busy dismissing them as vermin in the attic or walls, it had been straightforward, ordinary. Now that she'd heard the sound herself, it didn't seem ordinary at all.

Because for some reason the only mental image that had come to her mind when she heard the noise was that of a hand, a weakening hand, scratching helplessly for escape.

And that went from beyond imaginative to downright creepy.

Still, she was a practical woman, inclined to deal with problems in pragmatic ways. The ghastly horror-movie mental image had undoubtedly arisen from a mind still half-asleep and the fact that it was dark and the house was empty.

Even pragmatic people could occasionally suffer from imagination.

She sipped more cocoa and looked around, for the first time noting that she was in a living room that appeared as if it had been put together by a decorator. Few, if any, living rooms around these parts looked like that.

"Did you actually buy all your furniture to match?" she asked.

He seemed a little surprised, then laughed. "It happened that way. Not exactly a plan."

"How so?"

"Well, I'd been living here a couple of months when I realized I no longer wanted to live like a college student, sleeping on a sleeping bag and eating standing at my kitchen counter. I even had the amazing desire to be able to sit down."

"And?"

"And then I realized I had neither the time nor the patience to furnish the place piece by piece. So I headed out to one of those big furniture stores in Casper, whipped out my plastic and said I'd take this room, that room…whatever suited me that wasn't too expensive."

She laughed. "Have you caught up with the plastic?"

"Ages ago. I was impatient, not profligate. Even so, it ran so counter to my upbringing that I felt a bit disgusted with myself for a while. But…it saved time, I can relax now, and…there's even a chance the furniture will survive until the warranty runs out."

"It looks in pretty good condition to me."

"One man doesn't put much wear on most of it. I use so little of it, actually, unless I have guests. But at least I feel like I'm walking into a home. You don't have much at your place, do you?"

She shrugged. "Honestly? With the renovations, that's the last thing I'm worried about. Back in Denver there's a storage room full of furniture. Most of it stuff Don and I inherited from our families. We used it and often talked about how we liked antiques."

He had just sipped his own cocoa and now peered over his mug at her. She felt a trickle of something she didn't want to name, for fear of where it might lead her. But damn, he was attractive, and those dark eyes of his seemed to hold entire universes in them.

"Why," he asked, "do I get the feeling that saying you liked antiques wasn't exactly true?"

"Well, it's not that I don't like antiques. It's just that we had such a hodgepodge, and I was always spending time refinishing and mending, and back then the only time I had for that was when I was already tired. I think sometimes I resented it. And nothing, but nothing, was exactly right for where it was."

"What do you mean?"

"I took some design classes while I was getting my degree. You could say it permanently affected my eye. I'd look around our place and think, oh that piece is too big for that corner, or looks too small on that wall or, or, or. I couldn't quite get it all into an arrangement that satisfied me. So Don used to tease me that I was always moving furniture. And I was. And sometimes I seriously considered moving it all onto the street and replacing it completely."

He chuckled. "But now? When you finish this house? You said you might live in it. Will it fit there?"

"Some pieces will. The rest I may leave in storage for Colleen. The truth is, we're not talking priceless antiques here. Antiques, yes, priceless no. Well-worn hand-me-downs is more like it. So the question is really whether I feel some emotional attachment to a piece. Other than that..." She shrugged.

Having a conversation like this in the middle of the night seemed about as sane as running out of her house because of a noise. She stifled a yawn, feeling her eyes tear up, and realized that Mike had calmed her enough to sleep. Even the worsening storm seemed only to provide a soothing background.

Dimly she was aware of him spreading a blanket over her. The couch was so comfy, she just snuggled in a bit more.

Sleep, it seemed, had caught her between one breath and the next.

Chapter 5

She opened her eyes to the deep rumble of thunder, a rolling sound that seemed to come from afar, pass through the house and move on. Dim, gray light filtered through the curtains, hardly bright enough to be called day.

But she could smell the aromas of cooking bacon and coffee, and after she rubbed her eyes, she sat up and prepared to face a new day.

Her dreams, remembered only vaguely, had been troubled somehow, but they left little in their wake except uneasiness. Meaningless, and probably the result of sleeping in a strange house on someone's couch rather than in her own bed. Or even the remnants of what now seemed like a silly fear because she had heard an odd sound in her house.

When had she become afraid of sounds?

Sighing, she guessed her way to the bathroom. It

wasn't as if there was any place to get lost in a house with the shotgun floor plan. Somewhere between the front door and kitchen, a bathroom would open off the hallway. Or it would open off the kitchen. It was not as if she needed a marked trail.

Someone had evidently renovated at some point because just after she passed what appeared to be Mike's bedroom, she found the bathroom, a clearly recent addition from sometime in the past fifteen or twenty years. She did what she could with fingers, a washcloth and a bar of soap, then continued down the hall to emerge in a large kitchen with so many windows she would have bet that at one time it had actually been a porch. But that was the way these houses grew.

Mike stood at the stove, holding a fork, as bacon sizzled. This morning he wore some very old jeans, ragged at the cuffs and almost worn through at the seat, and a black T-shirt. When he heard her, he turned with a smile and she saw the yellow-and-red pattern on the front of his T-shirt, a spiral with a hand imprint on it and the words beneath it: The Sacred Circle of Life.

"Oh, I like that," she said.

He looked down. "It's from my high school. I buy a lot of my tees and sweatshirts from them because it helps support the school."

"I'll have to look into it. Colleen would probably love a shirt like that. Well, maybe a hoodie. Those seem to be her favorites."

"I don't recall if they have hoodies, but they also have other designs to choose from. How'd you sleep?" He turned back to the pan and began forking the strips of bacon onto a paper towel.

"I must have keeled over like a felled tree. The last

thing I really remember was talking to you." And him spreading a blanket over her. That little act of caring seemed hugely important somehow. Which was probably a measure of how little caring she'd been feeling in her life.

"You did kind of drop out practically mid-sentence. Grab a chair. Coffee?"

"Thanks. But first I need to check my cell." She hurried back to the living room to get the phone from her purse and came back while scanning it. No calls.

"I don't think I heard it ring," Mike remarked as he started cracking eggs into the pan.

A fresh mug of coffee sat on the table and Del sat before it, lifting it with pleasure. "Mmm, this smells so good. No, I didn't have any calls. But with Colleen, I'm almost compulsive about checking."

"I would be, too. Actually, I am. You never know when there might be an emergency."

"Do you get many?"

"Too many. Well, too many in the sense that some animal is hurt or suffering. Not too many to handle."

"So you're on call all the time?"

He smiled over his shoulder. "Where's the other vet?"

"Seems like the last one moved on five years ago or so."

"Seems like. This kind of practice isn't for everyone. For me, though, it just feels like a continuation of what I've been doing since I was knee-high to a grasshopper."

Del hardly tasted breakfast, although she tried to show her appreciation for it by eating an amount that wouldn't insult him. But her stomach was tightening, and anxiety was beginning to push at her.

She needed to arrange for Aunt Sally to look after Colleen. And then she had to get to work tearing out those walls because she wanted that noise *gone*. Bad enough it had unnerved her, but she didn't want it to bother Colleen any longer. Now that she had heard it herself, she was more than ever convinced that a creature of some sort lived in her walls.

Mike picked up on her uneasiness before they even finished. "You don't have to sit here on the edge of your chair," he said kindly.

She felt her cheeks heat. "I'm sorry. I'm not trying to be rude."

"I know. You're worried. And I meant what I said last night. If you want, Colleen and your aunt can stay here today so she's close and you don't have to worry."

"That's very generous of you." But still she thought she heard a note of reluctance in his voice. "I don't want to put you out. I…" Then she hesitated. How could she draw attention to a mere feeling she got about him without insulting him? Especially when he'd been nothing but helpful and understanding.

But Mike wouldn't let her go to her corner. "But? I hear a *but* there. Would you rather your daughter not stay in a redskin's house?"

Del gasped. She felt as if he had just punched her in the solar plexus. An eon passed before she could find the breath to whisper, "That thought never crossed my mind. What in the world…?"

He looked down at his plate. She could see his jaw work as if he were clenching his teeth. She didn't know whether to be furious or concerned. Everything inside her felt as if she'd been blindsided by a truck.

"Mike?"

He glanced to the side, away from her, then finally brought his dark gaze back. "I am," he said with an edge, "leaping to an all-too-familiar conclusion."

Then she knew exactly what to feel: sickened. She balled her paper napkin and threw it on the plate. "How dare you judge me? I'm no bigot." Then she shoved back her chair and marched down the hall to the front door.

Just before she reached the front door, she heard him call her name. Part of her wanted to just keep walking. She had seldom in her life felt so offended. But another part of her insisted she hear him out. He had, after all, been kind and helpful. He was still the man who had invited her into his home and spread a blanket over her as she slept.

Slowly, reluctantly, she turned to face him. He stood on the far side of the living room, his hands knotting and unknotting as if he didn't know quite what to do with them.

"I'm sorry," he said. "Sometimes I overreact."

"Maybe you have reason," she acknowledged. "I don't know. How would I? But I can tell you this—I've felt your reluctance since I found you talking with Colleen the other day. I don't know why you keep offering to help if it's not what you want to do. But I know one thing for certain—I don't want grudging help from anyone."

With that, she turned, grabbed her purse and marched out into the storm.

She hardly noticed the raging elements, even though it was unusual to have a storm go on for so long. The air was so full of electricity that she could almost feel it, and the raindrops were huge, striking her like a pelting of pebbles.

She didn't care. Whatever Mike's problems were, she wasn't going to let him treat her that way, accusing her of a bigotry she didn't feel even in the remotest parts of her brain or heart. Tarring her because his reluctance and hesitation kept making her wonder if his offers of assistance were genuine or forced.

She had quite enough trouble in her life, though she seldom allowed her to think of things that way. But Colleen required her all, and making a life for them, one that would guarantee that at some future time Colleen would have the care she needed, would be able to go to college and live as a reasonably independent adult, took every bit of energy she had.

She certainly didn't have much left over to tiptoe through Mike Windwalker's personal booby traps.

But then she reached the door of her house. And as she stood there, sheltered by the porch roof from the storm, she felt her shoulders sag a little. Maybe she should just dump this house for whatever she could get out of it. Maybe she shouldn't try to rescue it. After all, it scared Colleen and had even managed to scare her.

And what was this stuff about the house being sad? Mike had said that twice. What the hell did he mean?

All she knew was that where a few days ago she had loved the place, had seen it full of possibilities, now she felt an urge to just get rid of it, ditch it and move on.

And that was so unlike her as to be unnerving in itself.

She gave herself a shake and pawed through her purse for her keys. Damn it, where were they? The thought that she might have left them at Mike's made her want to beat her head on the closed door in front of her.

Good God, what was going on with her? She never reacted this way to minor frustrations. Never.

"Here."

She jumped and found Mike beside her, holding out her keys. So she had left them there. She snatched them. "Thanks." She jammed the key in the lock, twisting it.

"I'm sorry," he said.

"Probably," she agreed shortly. She twisted the key again, wondering why the bolt wasn't moving. "Damn it!"

A strong, warm hand reached out, covering hers. She yanked her hand back and Mike turned the key. This time the bolt clicked.

He threw the door open and she hurried inside, hoping he'd just go home, at least until she sorted through the internal storm that had come out of nowhere. Even as she was going off like a rocket, she wondered why. This was so unlike her.

She was stable. She had to be stable. How else had she gotten through losing Don, seeing Colleen paralyzed, all the work and stress and worry…?

She put her hand to her mouth, as if it would hold this mess of feelings inside, and tried to tell herself she hadn't gotten enough sleep last night, she'd been scared by a noise, silly or not, then insulted. Of course something had snapped.

And of course, it hardly helped that she was doubting her own sanity this past week because of the way she kept losing track of things.

But then strong arms closed around her and drew her

comfortingly against a hard chest, and a hand rubbed her shoulder as a voice murmured, "I'm sorry. I'm really, truly sorry. Don't cry."

Lord, she couldn't be crying. She never cried.

But she also hadn't realized just how damn tired she'd grown of being strong, independent, cheerful and so very, very alone.

She resisted the comfort he offered, but only for a few seconds. God help her, she needed to be held, even if only for a few minutes. She needed another pair of shoulders besides her own. Just for a few minutes. Just for a teeny slice of time.

Just for now.

She let herself weaken, let herself lean on his physical strength, gave in to the amazing feeling of arms around her, holding her. But the tears dried quickly, and in their wake came shame at her own weakness. She was stronger than this. She'd been proving it for a few years now. Surely she couldn't break over nothing. Because really, it was nothing. Nothing at all compared with what she'd been through.

She sniffled and pulled away, hating the loss of his embrace almost as much as she hated her moments of weakness. "Sorry," she said, turning away as she scrubbed her eyes. "I don't usually do this."

"Somehow I suspect you never do this."

She was afraid to look at him, afraid that if she did she'd fly right back toward the illusion of comfort his arms gave her. Because it *was* only an illusion. Mike Windwalker had barely set foot in her life, and everything about him suggested he was unlikely to remain.

"No," she said. "I don't."

Silence. She drew a deep breath, grasping for her inner strength. She looked around the foyer, trying to remind herself of all she needed to do, all she wanted to do to this house, and that she really didn't hate it, and everything would be fine because it *had* to be.

But her usual mantras failed her.

"I'm just tired," she said, as much to herself as him.

"It was a disturbed night," he agreed.

And finally she felt able to face him. He stood just inside the open doorway, as if waiting for an invitation to enter.

"Why don't you come in," she said, her voice sounding a bit thick, "and then maybe you can explain what we were fighting about?"

"Not exactly a fight." But he stepped inside and closed the door.

And at once she noticed the way the storm-created darkness seemed to close in. She didn't like it.

"Let's go to the kitchen," she suggested. "At least there's plenty of light in there."

He followed her and sat facing her at the table. She put her purse down beside her and pulled out her cell phone, setting it where she could reach it if Colleen called. If she knew anything about her and Mary Jo, though, the girls had probably spent most of the night giggling and watching movies, and they probably wouldn't even stir before noon.

With the overhead fluorescent fixtures on, the room was bright, although not yet cheerful. But at least the light held the shadows at bay.

Automatically she glanced around to make sure nothing had been disturbed. It bothered her at some level that she felt the need to do that. But right now there seemed to be more important things to contend with.

"What happened," he said, "was that I was reacting to a lifetime of experience. Perhaps unfairly."

"Definitely unfairly," she told him. "I already said I wasn't a bigot, yesterday."

"Saying it and feeling it can be two different things."

She studied his face, feeling truly curious about this man. But she didn't know how to ask, wasn't sure questions would be welcome. "I guess you would know about that better than I would."

A mirthless smile lifted one corner of his mouth. "Yeah, I would. In these parts anyway."

"I've heard the comments all my life," she admitted. "I was raised to consider them wrong. We're all human beings."

He nodded. "So when you seemed reluctant to let Colleen and your aunt stay at my place today, I interpreted it through a lifelong lens."

She nodded. "Okay. But I wasn't objecting. My problem is the way you seem so reluctant and hesitant even when you're being helpful. I feel like you don't want to be."

"Part of me doesn't."

"Then why offer?"

"Sometimes my better angels take control." He sighed, giving a little shake of his head. "I don't know if I can get you to understand. But I've been reluctant because of the possibility of people talking about you and Colleen. I'm used to what they say about me. I just don't want the two of you to get any of that crap."

"I'm tempted to say that this whole discussion sounds

like something that belongs in the Dark Ages, but I guess for you it's much more recent than that."

"Very much so. Most people don't say it to my face anymore. At least not around here, although the closer you get to a reservation, the more likely you are to have the stuff right in your face. But it's here, too."

"I know. I probably just don't hear most of it because on a few occasions I've told people to stop it."

He nodded. "Thanks. But it's still there. And I'm hesitant because it could bounce back on you and Colleen if you hang around with me too much."

"Well, too bad. If people want to treat us differently because we like you and spend time with you, then I don't want to know them."

"I've heard that before."

She heard the tinge of bitterness in his tone, and she longed to ask what had happened. But she hardly knew this man. How could she tread into what was clearly a serious sore spot? Finally she asked the question in a way he could misinterpret if he chose. "Mike?"

He sighed and put a hand to his face, rubbing his eyes with thumb and forefinger. It was almost a gesture of denial. But at last he dropped his hand. "You remember the vet I told you about? The one who mentored me?"

"Yes, of course."

"Well, he had a daughter."

And suddenly she could see it coming. Her stomach seemed to flip over. "You don't have to tell me."

"Maybe I do. Young love is foolish. I should have known better when she started flirting with me. I'd heard most of the insults by then, and I'd learned I wasn't welcome in a lot of places. I'd even been in a few fights with others my age who objected to me wandering off the rez. But maybe, in a way, I'd been sheltered, too, because I lived on the rez and went to school on the rez. God knows what I was thinking. Anyway, she finally asked me to take her to a movie. I was already getting teenaged crazy about her, if you know what I mean."

She nodded. "I remember that age well."

"I warned her people would talk. She said she didn't care. And maybe she thought she wouldn't."

"Maybe."

"I don't know how to explain it all. We were both eighteen, young, subject to peer pressure, I guess. We went out a couple of times, and her dad didn't *seem* to mind, although in retrospect I wonder if he didn't just keep silent because he figured she'd come to her senses pretty quick."

"That's awful!"

"I don't know what he thought. Or why he didn't tell her to stay away from me until later. Anyway, one night we were coming out of the movies and a group of guys attacked me. They made it pretty clear what they thought of me dating a white girl. I tried to fight back. I'm a fairly good scrapper, but there were more of them than me. And when they finally got me down on the ground, she joined them in kicking me and calling me names."

"Oh, my God!" Del's stomach cramped. "Oh, Mike!"

He shook his head. "It's done. But after that I don't find it easy to trust what people say about not caring what others think. And after that I wasn't welcomed at the vet's either. He told Livvie to stay clear of me. As if I wanted any more to do with her after that. As for her kicking me, too…well, maybe she was scared. I don't know. I never asked."

"And maybe the vet was protecting both of you by insisting she stay away."

"Maybe. I'll never know. But anyway, the point is…" He stopped.

"The point is you've got plenty of reasons to hesitate and be suspicious." She looked down at her hands. They were toughened hands, not exactly feminine with all the nicks, calluses and very short nails. But they were hands she was proud of and had no desire to conceal. She'd earned them. And as she looked at them she knew something else about herself all the way to the core. She lifted her eyes to Mike.

"I meant what I said," she told him. "This whole damn county can shun me, but I'm not going to shun you. And I'm old enough to be sure that I mean what I say."

His expression lightened, although it didn't fully become a smile. He didn't answer directly though. "When are we going to start tearing out walls?"

She almost put her head in her hand. "You know…"

"Yes?"

"That was an easy thing to threaten last night. This morning it's more complicated."

"How so?"

"Judging by the fact that noises seem to be in Colleen's room, I'd need to rip out the walls in there. Which means making a safe place somewhere else for her in the meantime."

"Ah. Okay, so we start by moving her. The dining room?"

It was a lot farther from the single downstairs bathroom, but it was also the only other room on the lower floor that she hadn't started tearing the walls out of. And it had the advantage of being on the other side of the house from where the noises were.

"That'll have to be it. I don't have any other options."

"So let's get to it."

Moving Colleen's belongings into the dining room proved to be the easy part of the job, and Mike's help was more than welcome. Not only was he strong, but he had a good eye. Before she had to tell him, he had already figured out exactly where to hang the bar over Colleen's bed so that she could maneuver in and out. In an hour, they had everything moved.

Del called a halt at the posters, though. They removed them from the bedroom, but she didn't want to rehang them. "I'll let Colleen tell me where she wants them now."

Mike nodded and laid them carefully on the bed.

They took a coffee break while Del called Beth to find out how the girls were doing. "Out like lights," Beth responded cheerfully. "Relax, Del. I'll let you know when she's ready to come home."

A call to her aunt ensured that Sally was able to come over at any time to keep an eye on Colleen.

Then she gave Mike a mask and goggles, and they went into Colleen's now-empty bedroom. First she sealed off the bathroom with plastic sheeting, then they picked up hammers and began to knock plaster loose. Before long, even with windows open and fans blowing, the plaster dust built into a nearly blinding cloud. Outside the storm continued to dump rain, which seemed only to hinder the escape of the dust.

Except every now and then a contrary gust would blow by, the dust would seem to freeze midair for an instant and then would change direction, being sucked out by the wind.

With two people it didn't take all that long. Finally they were able to stop, exhausted, and look at the heaps of cracked plaster on the floor. Only a few small pieces still clung to the lath.

Mike looked at her from behind his goggles as dust slowly settled. "That lath is so pretty I'd be tempted to sand it, varnish it and leave it."

"I've thought about it a time or two," Del admitted. "Those old-timers sure had a passion for covering up wood." Reaching out with a gloved hand, she tested some of it and found it sturdy. "The only problem is, I'm now looking at a wood wall instead of a plaster one. Admittedly it has more chinks, but still, I can't see through it." And wires were now exposed.

She crouched to look at them. "Well, it's what I expected. This whole house was apparently wired at the same time."

"Not up to code?"

"Far from it. I wondered when I bought it. In most of these old houses the wiring is outside the walls, but not this one."

"Money," he said, referring to his earlier remark about the house. "You know, it would be really interesting to look into the history of this place."

"Yeah, it would." She worked her fingers into the chink between two strips of horizontal lath and pulled plaster out. The spaces were essential so that the plaster would seep through and hold in place until it dried. The seepage she now pulled at was called a key. At the very least sixty or seventy years old, it crumbled.

She straightened, blowing a long breath. "Okay. Since it's raining so hard, I guess we leave the plaster on the floor. In the meantime I need to remove some of the lath so I can see what's going on back there."

Mike, too, touched the wall. "This seems like awfully high-quality wood to use as a backing for plaster."

"Yeah. Who knows? Maybe it was all they could get in a timely fashion. Or maybe someone had money to burn. Obviously, it wasn't built to be a bare wall, or it wouldn't have so much space between the laths."

He pulled down his mask, revealing a nose and mouth that were unsullied by the pale dust, and grinned. "I didn't realize tearing apart a house could feel like a treasure hunt."

She laughed. The hard work had eased the last of the tension from her mind and body. "It can be interesting."

Then he looked down at the oak floor. "Tell me you don't have to rip this up." He tapped it with his foot.

"No, you can see the floor joists directly under it from the basement. The ceiling will have to go, though, if we don't find the problem."

He looked up. "Well, it doesn't look as nice as the walls did. Has it been papered over?"

"At least a couple of times. Something else I'll never understand." She reached up, pointing to a seam. "Whoever did the job didn't match the seams. You can see them everywhere in the house. Lengths of paper overlay others. And then somebody painted on top of that."

"I was always told not to do that."

"Good advice. Paint on paper seldom looks good. It just seems to highlight the inconsistencies in the wallpapering. But you have the same problem with drywall, which is why you'll see me texture these walls before I paint them, unless I decide to paper them. I'm just enough of a perfectionist not to want to see shadows on walls where the wallboard is a little bent, or if the mudding shows through. Want some coffee?"

Colleen called while the coffee brewed, begging permission to stay with Mary Jo until that evening. Beth insisted she would enjoy it as much as the girls.

"Thanks," Del said finally, when she was sure it wouldn't be an imposition. "I've been tearing Colleen's room apart and moving her."

Silence. Then, "Colleen said something about hearing noises."

"Yeah. And last night I heard them, too. So you can tell her I'm going to get rid of the vermin if I have to tear out every wall in this house."

Beth laughed. "I'll do that. And if you want her to stay overnight, I can just drop by to get some clothes for her. The place must be a dusty mess."

"That's an understatement."

"Okay, when John gets back from Carl's ball game, I'll run over. I can do everything except get her to school in the morning. And I don't mind at all."

There it was again, that feeling of being cared for. Del felt her throat tighten just a bit and wondered how she'd managed for so long to overlook such little acts of kindness. Maybe because recognizing them made her feel weak? And she couldn't afford that. Ever.

When she closed her phone, the coffee was ready and

she realized she was hungry. "Something to eat?" she asked Mike.

"Tell you what. I'll run over to Maude's and pick us up a heart attack. I think we're working hard enough to survive steak sandwiches and fries."

"That does sound good. But have some coffee first. If your throat is as coated with dust as mine, you need to drink something before it all turns to plaster again."

He laughed but didn't linger, downing the coffee quickly. Then, covered in dust except for his face, forearms and hands, which he'd wiped down with a damp dish towel, he set out, promising to return quickly.

And that left Del alone in the house again. Hell. At least the growl of the storm had receded into the distance, although she could still see lighter rain falling. After calling Sally to tell her she wouldn't be needed today after all, she returned to work.

Taking a flashlight and a pry bar with her, she headed back to Colleen's room. While she waited for Mike, she could take down some of that lath. If experience was any guide, age should have caused the wood to shrink enough to make pulling out nails relatively easy.

She didn't want to use the lights in here now, either. Pulling all that plaster might have damaged wiring.

She started near the bottom, the place where she'd most likely find animal leavings if there were any. Three boards came off quickly, shedding more dust and making her sneeze and cough. "Keys" fell to the floor along with the boards, sending up small clouds. She should have worn her mask, but right now she was more concerned about finding something. Anything that would explain that darn noise.

She pulled one more board, finding it somewhat more difficult, then leaned in as far as she could, the flashlight on and sideways.

The gap between inner and outer walls was bigger than the norm. Whoever had built this house had used six-inch studs rather than the two-by-fours that were common in later construction. Another mystery. Mike was right. She ought to look into who had built this house, because they had made some interesting choices. The studs were also set farther apart, not the sixteen inches most common in modern building. Well, of course, with sturdier studs, you could make that trade-off.

And she couldn't see a darn thing that looked like rodent droppings or a rodent nest. If anything had ever lived in this wall, its leavings had long since turned to dust.

"Del?"

Startled by the unexpected voice, she jerked and banged her head. A moment later, eyes watering from pain, she sat on the floor looking up at her plumbing contractor, Edgar Dorset.

"Sorry," he said. "I thought you heard me come in."

She set the flashlight down and rubbed her head. "It's okay. What's up?"

"I couldn't remember if you wanted me tomorrow. I've got a job in Laramie, but I can put it off till Tuesday."

She looked up at the man, taking in his slightly plump figure, his "Sunday" clothes, his round face and balding head.

She *had* wanted him tomorrow because she was concerned about getting Colleen's bathroom whipped into shape. But now with the wall business… "It's okay, Edgar. It can wait a few days. If a few days is all you need."

"Oh, I can be here Tuesday." He indicated the wall with a jerk of his head. "Something going on?"

"I think I've got vermin."

"That's no fun. I had a rat die in my wall three years ago."

"I'm trying to avoid that."

"I can sure understand why." He squatted beside her and peered into the dark opening. "There's plenty of room. Have you considered trying to smoke it out?"

"I don't know. I mean this lath is so old it's probably tinder."

"Good point." He settled back a bit and smiled. "I'll think about it while I'm in Laramie. There's got to be some way to deal with this short of tearing the house down."

"You'd think."

He chuckled and stood. "See you Tuesday then, Del. Eight sharp?"

"As always. Say, if you run into Jimmy—" Jimmy was her electrical contractor "—tell him I might need him soon. Ripping out these walls might have damaged some of the wiring."

"I'll maybe see him tonight. It might be Sunday, like my wife says, but we play poker anyway."

"I don't know why it would offend the Lord more on Sunday than any other day."

His eyes twinkled. "That's my feeling. Seems like he said it was a day of rest. That's how I rest. Hannah don't always agree with that."

She could believe that. And she had wondered more

than once if Hannah had been born with a prune face. But whatever her disapproval of Edgar's poker, she loved the man to death. That much was clear.

"How soon do you need Jimmy?"

"Well, nothing seems to be shorted, so I think I can get by for a day or so just by not turning on lights in here. But I need to be sure."

"Absolutely. You still thinking about tearing out that wall in the basement?"

"Eventually." She looked at the hole she had just made in the lath and sighed. "Of course, if I can't find the vermin here I may have to go at it sooner. That brick wall seems to be right beneath us."

"True." He rubbed his chin. "I'll mention that to Jimmy, too. Unlikely that wall isn't flush up against the basement wall, though, so I'd be surprised if you'd find anything behind it. But if you decide you need to pull it out, the two of us can help." He winked. "Some things can always use an extra strong back."

She returned his smile, but she wasn't exactly wet behind the ears. Both Jimmy and Edgar could always use extra work, even if it was carting bricks out of the basement. The offer of help would come with a bill attached. Not that she would blame them for that. They all had families to support and bills to pay.

Edgar took his leave, but just as Del was about to pry loose some more lath, she heard Mike call her from the kitchen.

"Del? Lunch is here and it's hot."

The news caused a Pavlovian response. At once her stomach growled and her mouth started watering. Straightening, she automatically brushed her dusty hands against her jeans, then realized the jeans were even dustier. *Duh.* Just another sign of lack of sleep.

She washed up at the kitchen sink and joined Mike at the table where he'd set a couple of foam containers and two tall soft drinks with straws. When she opened her container, the incredible smell of the steak sandwich and fries reached her nose and she drew it in with pleasure.

"Colleen would be so upset if she saw me eating this."

"Why?"

"Because we have to watch what she eats. She's… less active now, obviously."

Mike's gaze softened. "That has to be tough."

"At her age? You better believe it. But she's pretty good about it most of the time. Every now and then we break the rules. But mostly we have to eat healthy stuff."

He looked down at his sandwich. "I don't think the sandwich is all that unhealthy. But the fries…" He shook his head. "I'm always having to tell dog owners that if they want to share fries with their pooch, one fry is plenty. They're not big enough, most of them, to justify human-size servings."

Del grinned. "I don't think I've heard it put that way before."

"Neither have a lot of dog owners." He smiled at her, then lifted his sandwich. "We all want to pamper our pets. I'm a sucker for it myself. Those big sad eyes, that wagging tail…hard to say no to. But for most dogs, if you're going to break down, a taste is more than enough. Heck, you can even give your dog a piece of chocolate-chip cookie. But just a piece."

"I thought chocolate was poison to them."

"It can be, if they get enough of it, and what constitutes enough is based on their body size. What would kill a Chihuahua obviously wouldn't kill a Great Dane."

She bit into her own sandwich, savoring it. "Thanks so much for this. It's wonderful."

"You're more than welcome. I'm not exactly being generous here. I've been thinking about one of these all morning. Did I see Edgar Dorset leaving when I pulled up?"

"Yeah. He was supposed to do some plumbing for me tomorrow but he got offered a job in Laramie and wondered if I could wait until Tuesday. Considering this whole process just took a sharp, unexpected turn, I can wait on the plumbing for a day. He was nice though. He said if I needed help with the brick wall in the basement, he and Jimmy would be glad to lend their backs." She smiled. "Invoice attached, I'm sure."

"I'm sure. Who's Jimmy?"

"Jimmy Morton. He's my electrician."

Mike's brow knit. "I don't think I've met him."

"Well, I don't usually see him about much. He seems like a lonely man, actually, but then my only contact with him is when he's working. I guess he and Edgar play poker together, so maybe I'm all wet." And how normal and natural it seemed to be sitting here gossiping about other folks in the county. It had been a long time since she'd done that.

She rolled her shoulders to loosen muscles and reached for another fry. Oh, the sin! Colleen would surely kill her if she found out. She looked up to find Mike's attention was focused on his meal, which gave her a few moments to study him.

And once again she felt the pull of attraction. He was a magnificently attractive man and she wondered if he even realized it. Probably not, as skittish as he was.

But it had been a long time since she'd noticed a man that way, and she decided not to fight it. Mike would evidently fight it enough for both of them if he happened to feel the same attraction.

But she found herself enjoying the way his muscles moved under his black—well, it had been black this morning, but now it was so full of plaster dust it looked more like a dark gray—T-shirt. And he was unquestionably handsome. Hadn't she once heard someone say that the Cheyenne were beautiful people?

As soon as the thought crossed her mind, she pulled back from it. There was a judgment in that statement, regardless of who had said it and how it was meant. She looked down and bit her lip, realizing that Mike probably had ample reason to be wary, especially if thoughts like that could occur to her. Maybe there was some of that ugliness buried deep in her own mind.

"Something wrong?" he asked.

"Not a thing." Not a thing except she had realized she'd picked up some mental lint she didn't want, and nothing, of course, except that she was starting to become too entirely aware that he was a man and she was a woman. The kind of awareness she had lost in the aftermath of tragedy.

An awareness she didn't need or want, at least not now. Her priorities had to lie in a different direction.

She hastened to eat another fry so he wouldn't find cause to question her again.

Just focus on the important stuff, she told herself.

Like Colleen and the noises in her room. No time to be remembering she was a woman with needs and wants. Not for at least a few years.

But she could still enjoy the view. The thought made her smile secretly. That much was allowed.

Chapter 6

The rain let up during the afternoon, so Mike helped her carry the chunks of plaster out to the huge commercial trash bin she kept in her garage. Whenever she filled it, she called the removal people to tow it away and leave her with a fresh one.

Removing the plaster proved even more time-consuming than knocking it off the walls in the first place. By the time they were done, it was late afternoon and more clouds were crowding in.

But Mike didn't look in the least tired. He knocked dust off himself and asked, "What next?"

"Frankly, if I don't find something in the walls, I don't know."

They went back into the house together, and Del started snapping on lights in the hallway, in the kitchen, even work lamps in the living room. The darkness of the day got to be a drag, and in some way made her edgy.

"Well," Mike said once light flooded all the down-stairs rooms except the one they had spent the day tearing apart, "we could try a campout."

She stopped and looked at him. "A what?"

"A campout. You've got the walls torn out. All the activity might have frightened the vermin away temporarily. So we could sit in that darn room tonight and just listen."

"I could also spray something in the walls to kill whatever it is and live with the odor."

"Weeks or maybe longer depending on how big it is."

"Damn." She stared down at her toes. "Well, it must be big."

"Why do you say that?"

"Because every now and then I find things moved after I've been out a little while. And some of the stuff isn't exactly lightweight."

She raised her gaze slowly and found him totally arrested, staring off into space.

Finally he said, "Why didn't you mention that before?"

"Because…well, it sounds nuts. It has to *be* nuts. I probably just don't remember where I put stuff."

"Maybe."

She wished she hadn't said anything. She didn't like the way he stared past her, as if he didn't want to meet her gaze.

But finally his dark eyes came back to her and he said quietly, "Have you considered the possibility that someone is trying to scare you?"

She gasped in shock. "Why would anyone…? Mike, that's crazy. That's paranoid!"

"Maybe so." He shrugged one shoulder. "But given the sounds, and given stuff being moved, I wouldn't be too quick to dismiss it."

She wanted to argue with him. She wanted to believe that he was seeing this whole thing through some level of distrust because of the way he had been treated.

But she had heard the sounds. Colleen had been frightened by them more than once. And things *had* been out of place. Just enough, and just often enough, that she had started to scan every room when she entered it after being gone for a while, sort of like a personal mental health test. *Did I remember correctly where I put it?* She'd even started to pay closer attention every time she put something down.

"Damn," she said, and took two steps so that she could sag onto the bottom step of the wide staircase. "Damn."

"I'm sorry." He sounded stiff. "I don't mean to upset you. That was thoughtless."

"Oh, stop it," she sighed. "Just stop it. Why would it be any crazier that someone might be trying to scare me than that I'm suddenly losing my ability to remember where I put things? I mean, the latter sounds like a bigger problem than the former."

"I could see how you might think that."

She shook her head. "But there's absolutely *no* reason for anyone to want to scare me. Nobody else would want this house in its current condition."

"Then I'm wrong."

But she couldn't quite agree. Losing her mind or being deliberately scared by someone. She preferred the latter, frankly. The thought that she was becoming forgetful had been bothering her. But if she went the other way, there was a question that had to be answered.

"Why did that thought occur to you?"

"I don't know." He spread his hands. "Random brain misfire? Psychic intuition? Maybe because I said something earlier about how tearing the walls out felt like a treasure hunt?"

She started to nod thoughtfully. "I guess that makes a kind of sense. I suppose someone might think there's something of value hidden in here."

"Oh, it's ridiculous." He turned, saw a wooden chair against a wall, and dragged it over, straddling it and folding his arms across the back so he was close and could look at her. He sighed. "It just popped out. In the first place, somebody would have to have a *reason* to think something of value is hidden here. Which would mean a former occupant, or relative of an occupant. And what would you say if someone came up to you and said, 'I think Grandma left her life savings in a tin can under the floor?'"

Almost in spite of herself, Del grinned. "Frankly, I'd tell them that if I found Grandma's savings, I'd give it to them."

"Exactly. Most people would do precisely that. So it's ridiculous to think someone would go to such great lengths to scare you out of the house. I mean, even if Grandma *did* leave her savings in here somewhere, it's unlikely to amount to more than a few hundred dollars. If it hasn't rotted away."

"True." But she couldn't fail to note the way he seemed to be talking himself out of the idea more than her. Yet he was the one who had brought it up. But he was also the one who had said the house felt sad.

"Brain misfire," he said again. "I must be watching too many true-crime shows or something."

"Well, as far as I know, the only things of value in here are my tools and supplies. I always lock the house so nobody gets tempted, but the most you could hope to walk out of here with, as long as I don't leave the house for long, is an expensive bunch of drill bits and socket wrenches. That kind of stuff. If anybody wants any more, I'll have to be away long enough for them to bring in a moving van." She shook her head. "Frankly, I worry more about bored kids getting in here and vandalizing things."

"Makes sense."

"Which brings us back to vermin in the walls. And I have to get rid of whatever it is, because I'll be damned if I let Colleen get scared at night." She sighed. "I don't know about you, but I'm getting tired. Time to call it a day."

"How about that campout I suggested? If we keep watch together, maybe we can pinpoint the sound."

"You mean sit up all night? That would kill tomorrow."

"Or take turns. Did it wake you last night?"

"Maybe. I'm honestly not sure. I was restless to begin with." Having dreams that would make her blush if she let herself recall them. She felt a faint coloring of her cheeks, probably not enough for him to notice.

"Is it waking Colleen?"

"Sometimes."

"Then maybe we can count on that. I've got a couple of sleeping bags we can use."

"Okay. It's worth a try." Just then she heard a car pull

up out front. "That must be Beth coming to get Colleen's clothes."

He rose immediately. "I'll just go home and shower and get those sleeping bags."

Then he made her heart ache: he went out the back door rather than the front, and she didn't doubt for a second that he did so in order to avoid being seen by Beth Andrews.

Despite what she had said, he still didn't want anyone to talk about her and Colleen because of him.

If she let herself think about it, she was quite sure she might have cried.

Mike crossed the backyards and let himself into his own house. And while he had backtracked from his suggestion that someone might be trying to frighten Colleen and Del, he wasn't sure he believed his own rationalization.

No, there was no logical reason to assume such a thing. At least not one he was aware of. That didn't mean it wasn't so.

Nor had the thought been a mere mental misfire. No, it had been an intuition. The kind of intuition he'd been taught as a child not to ignore.

Which left him with a huge cultural gulf he simply didn't know how to begin to bridge with Del. Most of the things his uncle had taught him as a child, most of the things he had experienced along those lines, were utterly dismissed by the European world. They had no room in their science for the spiritual or mystical.

So how could he even hope to explain it without convincing Del he was a nut?

He climbed into his shower, letting the hot water beat

away all the fatigue along with the day's dust. His past, he thought, not only lay behind him, but it very much lay between him and the world he had adopted.

Maybe he should have listened to his uncle when Walking Crow had told him that he was called, that when the animals spoke to him they were summoning him to be a medicine man. Instead, bullheadedly, he had refused to listen.

But when in his life hadn't he been torn at least to some degree? Torn between old ways and new ways, torn between his traditional beliefs and the ones he learned at school. While the parochial school had by his time learned to treat his tribal beliefs with respect, the inescapable teaching remained that there was only one true faith…and it wasn't the faith of the Morning Star People.

He'd melded it all somehow, and sometimes even felt comfortable with it. Until something happened like today, when intuitions rose and goaded him, and he could not ignore them. When the old ways told him one thing, and the logic of the new ways entirely another.

And sometimes he wished Walking Crow were still around, so he could pick up a phone and call his uncle and talk things over.

Something was going on here, but because he'd turned his back on the old ways to a large degree, he didn't know enough. Not nearly enough.

After he dressed in fresh clothes, he picked up the sleeping bags, left over from when he'd still been in school and he and some buddies had occasionally taken off for a weekend to hike and camp. He filled a canvas tote with snack foods because he didn't want to burden Del and headed back to her house. Across the backyards. Feeling a bit like a kid who was doing something wrong.

Stupid.

He found Del in Colleen's room. She had apparently had time to finish vacuuming the room and was now running damp rags over everything, one rag in each head.

Her face looked a little pinched and tired, and he felt badly for her. He doubted he had been anywhere near as much help as he might have been today.

He dropped everything on the clean floor and said, "Let me finish that. You run up and take your shower."

She barely managed a smile. "Sorry, I'm beat. And I can't wait to get this dust off. It's starting to rub me raw in a few places."

"Then go. You're not alone now. Shout if anything worries you. In the meantime, I'll just finish wiping stuff down for you."

It was easy to see where she had wiped and where he needed to finish up. He felt glad for the simple, mindless task. His thoughts had started to follow disturbing paths, paths that made him feel both mentally and physically edgy.

Finally he paused for a moment in his wiping and closed his eyes. Upstairs he could hear water running, and outside the night was deepening, punctuated by flashes of lightning. In here, a couple of flashlights were all that held darkness at bay.

And some of that darkness seemed to be seeping into him. Something was wrong in this house. Very wrong. And damned if he knew what.

And what an irony it would be if he proved unable

to help Del because he had a long time ago refused to follow the Red Road to become a medicine man.

Of course, had he done as his uncle wished, he wouldn't be here now either.

Sighing, he opened his eyes and resumed wiping at the walls and anything else that looked dusty. The air had cleared considerably, and a fan at the window still sucked the remaining dust out of the room.

And upstairs Del was naked in the shower. Tightening his mouth, he wiped harder. He couldn't afford to think about that. Couldn't allow himself the feelings and needs she so easily evoked in him.

What was wrong with him? Once wasn't enough to tell him where this would lead if he followed his desires?

And Del sure as hell didn't need this from him now, if she ever would. Right now, it was most important to get to the bottom of what was frightening Colleen. What had managed to frighten Del enough that he'd found her standing outside her own house in the dead of night, reluctant to return.

And he'd heard that damn sound himself. Clearly. More like weary fingers, nails short or gone, making a half-hearted attempt to get attention.

It sure hadn't sounded like animal claws. He had enough experience to know those sounds as intimately as the sound of his own breathing.

So what the hell was it?

Light suddenly bounced around the room and he turned quickly. Del stood in the doorway carrying a camp lantern, one of those battery-operated things with a fluorescent tube. She wore sweats again, but they seemed to caress her figure rather than conceal it. "Can you breathe?" she asked.

Oh, yeah, he could breathe, and right now he smelled a woman fresh from the shower, still warm from the heat of the water, scented with soap and shampoo. Her hair hung wetly, as if she hadn't bothered to dry it with more than a towel, and even in the light from that single lantern and the flashlight on the floor he could tell her skin was flushed a healthy pink.

And in that instant he wanted her so much that he gripped the damp towels in his hands until his fingers ached. Not even reminding himself of Livvie's taunts could batter down the sudden surge of aching need.

"Yeah," he managed to say, aware that his voice sounded oddly thick. He cleared his throat and looked away before he could make a fool of himself. "Yeah," he said again, more firmly, even though he was lying because right now it felt as if there wasn't any air left in the room, or in the entire universe. Primitive rhythms beat in his blood, in his loins. He forced himself to take another swipe at the walls.

"It doesn't have to be perfect," she said, coming into the room. "As long as we beat the dust down enough to breathe."

"Just a bit more." Just a few more swipes until his self-control mastered his more basic urges.

And offering to stay the night here had surely been one of the *stupidest* things he had done in a long time. He knew better, far better. This woman had a huge "off-limits" sign around her, practically painted in neon. Even if he removed the likelihood that she and her daughter might suffer for getting too close to him, there was her situation. He wasn't ignorant enough or selfish enough not to realize what she was up against already in her personal life. She didn't need additional complications of any kind. Least of all him.

So he finished wiping the wall, avoiding looking at her, avoiding the very thing he had set himself up for. Yeah, he needed to go beat his head on a wall until he managed to pound some sense into it, until his head ached so much more than his manhood. He needed to forget he wanted Del Carmody more than he'd wanted anything in a long time.

Behind him he heard her moving around. When at last he felt he had a leash on himself, he turned around to find she had spread the sleeping bags out. And she hadn't spread them on opposite sides of the small room. Oh, no. Somehow they were only a foot apart on the floor.

Did she have even the least idea?

No, probably not. Why would she? She obviously trusted him, and somehow he had to live up to that. Crap. Right now he had never felt less like living up to anything.

He cleared his throat again. "Where should I toss these rags?"

She came to him immediately and took them. "I'll just spread them on the washer until I'm ready to do a load. Use the bathroom there." She nodded to Colleen's bathroom, behind a closed door, and he headed in there.

The room showed signs of age and wear, with chipped tiles and a tub that looked as if it had seen better years. But just like the bath upstairs, the room was unusually large. People didn't build them like this anymore. No, you were lucky if you could squeeze into a modern bath.

He washed his hands and forearms and returned to the bedroom. Del was already sitting on one of the sleeping bags, and she offered a smile as he emerged.

"I really appreciate you being willing to do all of this," she said.

He hesitated only a moment, feeling like the wolf in *Little Red Riding Hood,* before sinking to sit cross-legged on the other sleeping bag. "It's what neighbors do," he answered, both seriously and to try to remind himself that that was their *only* relationship. Distance. He needed to keep the distance.

"Not every neighbor," she said. "This room isn't exactly crowded with helping hands."

He tightened his mouth and gripped his knees with his hands, keeping them safely occupied. "Maybe some aren't aware you could use some help."

At that her smile faded a bit. "True. I don't generally go waving my problems in people's faces. But I don't think you do either."

"No," he admitted.

"My husband always said I was cussedly independent. I'm not sure he always meant it as a compliment." Her face shadowed, but then she managed another smile. "Mostly I like the independence of doing my own thing. When I need help I hire it. But…this is different."

"We'll get to the bottom of it somehow."

"I have to. It's either that or move, and the way I've got this place torn up… Well, I suppose I could move us into the house I finished four months ago, but I'm trying to rent it."

"Do you need the income?"

"From the rental? It would help. I'm okay for now,

but there'll come a point when paying the mortgage on two houses will drain me."

He nodded. "It must be a load."

"Not when things go right." She unfolded her legs and stretched out on the sleeping bag on her side, her head propped on her hand. "I imagine your childhood was a lot different from mine."

"Life isn't *all* that different on the rez."

"I didn't mean it like that."

He felt an immediate pang of guilt. "Jumping to conclusions again."

"Yup." But she smiled at him. "Still, I grew up in the local culture. Your experience had to be somewhat different. For me, I guess the equivalent would have been being born to an immigrant family." She suddenly held up her hand, "And don't tell me you folks weren't the immigrants. I know that."

He chuckled because he had to. "Well, we were immigrants, too."

"Ah, but there was no one else here when you arrived."

"There's some debate about that, too."

Her interest clearly perked. "Really?"

He shrugged. "Depends on if we're being politically correct. Many of my people aren't pleased when others suggest we weren't here first. But there's some evidence in South America that a wave of immigration actually came around from Australia, long before the time dates given for my people. They may have reached as far north as Central America. And there are those Olmec heads."

"I've seen photos of them and always wondered."

"Other than to clarify prehistory in the Americas, I

think it's pointless to argue about it. My people clearly migrated here, too, whether it was twelve thousand years ago or twenty-five thousand."

"And apparently all of us came out of Africa."

"So it would seem. At this point, getting proprietary about things that happened so long ago seems like it should be of interest primarily to academics."

"Well, we *do* know who was here when the Europeans arrived."

He smiled slightly. "Indeed, whether it was the first group of Europeans, or the second, or the third…"

The way he said it made her laugh. "I guess that's another debate."

"Endlessly."

She appeared to hesitate then said, "If I'm treading on toes here, let me know. But you said a couple of things, and they got me curious. Like when you said this house is sad."

He should have anticipated this. It was bound to come. The question was how frank he wanted to be. And then he decided to just go for it. If she didn't like it, or treated it as merely interesting lore, what did it really matter? It would start drawing lines, and then he could stand behind them. Safely. Away from the temptation to repeat one of the biggest mistakes of his life.

"My uncle, Walking Crow, was a medicine man. He thought I should follow in his footsteps."

"Why? Tradition?"

Mike shook his head. "It's never tradition. It's about abilities. About being called to take a journey and learn things that aren't part of your kind of thinking."

"And you were called?"

"My uncle thought so. I was drawn to animals. I don't

recall my earliest experiences, but he told me when I got older that I shouldn't ignore the call of the wolf."

Del sat up. "Meaning?"

"I awoke night after night to find a wolf standing in my bedroom. Or so it seemed."

"Was it real?"

He hesitated. There was only so much he could share, as his people kept their beliefs very private. And with good reason, given how most non-natives reacted to them, either with disdain and disbelief, or some kind of New Agey cultism.

He spoke carefully. "In the terms of my people, it was real. It was a summons. But I refused to take the Red Road, and instead followed my own path."

Del leaned forward, intent. "Why did you refuse?"

"Because…" Again he hesitated. "Because the Red Road is a difficult one and would require a commitment I wasn't sure I wanted to make. By the time I finished kindergarten, I had conflicting worldviews. Maybe because I was young I wanted to follow the new ways, not the old ones."

She nodded thoughtfully, clearly interested in what he had to say. But how much could he say? He couldn't betray what his people chose to keep private.

"So what exactly do you mean by the Red Road?"

Ah, now there was a problem. He sought ways to explain to her without revealing matters he shouldn't share with an outsider. Finally, he sought refuge in the dry terms of anthropology. "Have you heard of the shamanic path?"

She shook her head. "Not really."

"Well, let me start by saying my people don't like the

word *shaman*. Mainly because it's a Siberian word and has been flung around rather liberally by academics."

"Okay."

"I'm just using it here because…well, you'd probably connect with its meaning better than if I resort to our preferred translation, which has plenty of baggage of its own."

"And that is?"

"Medicine man or woman."

"Spiritual leader, or healer?"

"Or both. Anyway, if you look into the subject you'll find the so-called shamanic path, or journey, is strikingly similar across cultures and continents. But the main thing to remember is that it's a journey. It's not something you do once—you do it all your life."

"That *is* a commitment."

"And it's not easy. It involves suffering, sacrifice and a willingness to look into other realities that can be terrifying. Altered states of consciousness, if you prefer the clinical term. I may have been called, but I didn't answer. I learned one thing at home, and another at school, and finally I opted for what I was learning at school. I sidestepped into the so-called rational world."

Her brows lifted a bit. "Why do you say *so-called?*"

"Because mysteries and spirituality exist whether science can explain them or not. This *rational* world denies those experiences and calls them hallucinations."

She nodded slowly, absorbing what he was saying. He gave her credit for not arguing with him. "I get the feeling you regret your choice."

"Once in a while. But not often. I mostly feel that I'm doing what I was meant to do."

"That's a good feeling to have."

She was letting him out of the noose of tightening questions, and he felt grateful to her. But at the same time, just talking about it raised the questions he'd never really answered for himself—like whether he had indeed made the right choice.

Del spoke. "It must have been a hard decision to make, to go against what your uncle thought you were called to do."

"There's nothing like being young and headstrong."

Another smile graced her face. "True. I was supposed to marry the son of the rancher next door, thus combining the two ranches. Clearly, I didn't live up to expectations."

"Did your folks object when you went off to college?"

"Pretty much. They figured I'd meet someone there and never come home to the ranch permanently. They were right. After my parents passed away, I sold the ranch to the rancher's son next door."

The way she said it made him chuckle. But he felt compelled to add, "I'm sorry about your parents."

"I miss them. What about you?"

"My parents are gone, too. Mom died last year. And my sister married a Seminole and they live in Florida now. I fly down to see them once a year."

"In the winter, I hope."

"Of course. If I'm going to take a trip to the Sunshine State it has to be in February or March, right about the time I've decided I'm going to hate the cold and snow forever."

"And it does start to feel like forever about then." She sighed a little, as if thinking about it, then said, "You've had an interesting life. Very different from mine."

"I could say the same for you."

She laughed. "I guess you could." Then she looked around at the shadowy room. "I'm starting to feel edgy."

"Any particular reason?"

She shook her head. "I wish. It's just a feeling."

"This whole house gives me feelings."

It must have been an opening she had been waiting for, because she immediately asked, "What did you mean when you said the house feels sad? What *exactly?* Some kind of mystical feeling?"

"I can't explain it." He wanted to evade her question, realizing that they were probably about to get into a conflict for which there could be no easy resolution. Yet he knew evasion would be exactly the wrong answer now. For them both. "It just feels to me as if this whole house is weeping for something."

"And you don't get that feeling in your house."

He shook his head slowly.

"Well, damn." All of a sudden she jumped up from the sleeping bag and hurried from the room.

He thought about sitting right where he was, waiting for her to deal with this however she needed to. Then he considered just how much that woman had on her plate, from strange noises in her house to a paralyzed daughter.

He couldn't do it. With a sigh, he rose and went to meet his fate head-on.

Chapter 7

Del stood in the kitchen, trying to make coffee even though she was shaking. She didn't know if she was mad, or if she felt he was trying in some way to con her, or what. Just because Mike Windwalker had been the vet in town for the past few years didn't mean he was someone she could trust.

All that stuff about being a medicine man. She had been willing to accept it as part of his cultural heritage, but now she wondered if he hadn't been making up stuff to try to impress her some way…or to scare her.

After all, it had been Mike Windwalker who had suggested that someone was trying to scare her out of her house. She couldn't imagine any earthly reason why anyone should want to do that, so why had that even popped into his mind? Because *he* was the one trying to scare her away?

"Del?"

"I don't want to talk right now." She almost spilled coffee as she scooped it into the filter.

"Then I'll talk. I'm sorry I upset you, but I can't pretend to be somebody I'm not."

She turned then to face him, seriously annoyed though damned if she was sure why. "And just what are you?" she demanded. "All this talk about feelings and shamanism, and then trying to scare me out of my house because you say it feels sad? I'm supposed to swallow that?"

His jaw dropped a little, and then his dark eyebrows drew together. "I'm not trying to scare you out of your house. In case you hadn't noticed, I've been busting my back trying to help you find out what's going on."

"Sure. And dropping little hints in my ear about feelings you get, about how somebody might be trying to scare me out of this place. Suggestions."

"They're not suggestions! I'm not trying to convince you of anything. I'm trying to help solve the problem."

"If they're not suggestions, what are they?" She wanted an answer, and it had better be a good one.

He looked away for a moment, then faced her again with a steady gaze. "They are what they are. Feelings. Intuitions. Something I was taught to be open to since my earliest childhood. This house speaks, for those with ears to hear, and you can like that or not. It doesn't change what I sense."

"Why would *you* sense it and no one else?"

"You already sense it. Your daughter has heard noises. You've heard them. *I've* heard them. Something is wrong with this house."

"There's plenty wrong with it. And I'm fixing what's wrong with it."

"But there's something you can't fix with all the hammers and nails in the world. If you think I'm trying to get you out of this house, if you *really* believe that, I'll leave now."

She couldn't immediately answer. For some reason what he had said had knotted her emotions in some way and she couldn't fully untangle the skein of feelings and thoughts. But as he started to turn away, clearly intending to leave, she knew one thing for certain.

"I trust you," she said. Words that came from her heart, more than her brain. Her brain kept saying she must be nuts, all this talk of intuition and feelings and the house speaking...

But her heart believed something very different.

He faced her again, slowly. Reluctantly. "Are you sure about that?"

She almost winced when she heard the edge of bitterness in his tone, and she knew where it came from. God, she felt about two inches tall. "Look, I'm not criticizing your heritage. Let's get that clear."

"Really?" He folded his arms.

"Really. But you're asking me to accept things I don't believe. You've lived in my world. I haven't lived in yours. So suppose you tell me how someone from *my* world is supposed to believe that this house is sad? That a house, an inanimate object, is capable of having feelings?"

"That'll take the Golden Gate Bridge, to span that gap." Again, an undercurrent of bitterness.

And that bitterness pierced her. The study of architectural engineering had *not* prepared her to cross culture gaps. It hadn't given her even the smallest of tools for dealing with the gulf that lay between them now. "Help me," she said finally. "I'll try."

Then she turned to finish making the coffee, letting him decide for himself whether to continue this conversation or leave. Because she just didn't know what to say next.

It was beyond any experience in her life.

When she had switched on the coffeemaker and washed her hands, she turned again from the counter and found Mike still standing there. Even in the bright fluorescent lighting, he somehow looked archetypal, mysterious. And in the course of this single evening, he had indeed become mysterious to her, no ordinary man with ordinary thoughts or an ordinary life. At least not the ordinary kind of man she was used to.

"In my culture," he said finally, "there are no inanimate objects."

She caught her breath. "What do you mean?"

"We believe that consciousness imbues everything. The stones, the earth, the air, the water, even this house. That storm outside, the wind, the fire, the lightning. All of it is aware. When we cut a tree we give thanks to it for its sacrifice. We thank the rocks when we use them to build a fire pit. We thank the rain for choosing to moisten our fields."

She nodded but remained silent, afraid of interrupting him. More than anything, she felt a need to understand him.

"This house is aware," he said flatly. "Not like you or I, but it *is* aware. And something has made it sad. It weeps. And if you want to know what my uncle would have said about it, I can tell you."

She nodded again.

"He would have said we need to find out what happened to sadden this place."

For long moments there was no sound but the distant rumble of thunder and the nearby sound of the coffeemaker. She stood there, trying to absorb what he was telling her, trying to fit his worldview into her own.

"I'm trying," she said finally.

"I know it's not easy. It's alien to you. I'm not even asking you to believe. Just telling you something about who and what I am. About how I see things."

She knew then that she had to cross that gulf somehow. Because if she didn't find a way, right now, Mike Windwalker would once again return to his private life, would once again become the hesitant, reluctant man she had first met.

But there were no words. She couldn't say she agreed with his beliefs. She couldn't, certainly not having just been exposed to them for the very first time.

So without words, all she could do was show him acceptance. She crossed the kitchen to him and put her arms tentatively around him.

"I'm sorry," she said. "I was frightened and confused."

And slowly, very slowly, he lifted his own arms and hugged her back. "You don't have to accept it," he said quietly.

"Yes, one way or another I do. Because accepting it is accepting you."

"That's a lot to ask of yourself."

"No, it's actually very little. I don't have to believe it. I don't have to see the world the same way you do. But I *do* have to respect your beliefs."

It seemed to her that his arms tightened, so she tightened her own around him. He smelled so good from his recent shower, and he felt so good against her. She wanted to believe that he could be a haven, however temporarily, because it had been so long, too long, since she had had one.

She recognized the weakness in herself, and knew that soon she would have to take up her burdens again, because they were *her* burdens. But she let herself feel, for just these few minutes, that she didn't have to shoulder them alone.

For one wild moment she wished she were just an ordinary woman herself, as free as a bird, but the instant she thought it, she felt guilty. Nothing could make her wish Colleen out of her life. Nothing.

So she stepped back and turned to pour coffee for them. "How," she asked, hoping her voice didn't sound as thick as it felt, "would we go about finding out why the house is sad?"

"Good question. My suggestion would be to find out what we can about previous owners, whether there were any tragedies."

Such a prosaic answer. What had she been expecting? That he would offer to seek a vision? Talk to the house? She could have laughed at herself if she hadn't already put her foot in it enough for one night.

"Okay," she agreed. "We can check the newspaper morgue in the morning. Or I can. I guess you need to be at work."

"Unfortunately. I have a full day scheduled. But you might save a lot of time by asking Velma, the dispatcher at the sheriff's office."

"I should have thought of that! Or Nate Tate. That

man must know about everything that's happened in this county in the past sixty years."

"Yeah, he probably would."

"I'll start there then, right after I take Colleen to school."

They carried their coffee into Colleen's former bedroom and settled onto the sleeping bags, sitting cross-legged and facing each other.

Again, Del felt as if something were trying to close in on her, something that hovered in the shadows beyond the camp lantern. And then a thought trickled across her awareness, a thought she usually ignored.

"You know, maybe the sadness you're sensing is me."

"Why do you say that?"

"Because, well, I'm sort of aware that my grief over Don was truncated because of what happened with Colleen. I had to focus all my attention on getting her through that. There was a counselor who worked with both of us for a while, and she said, basically, that the devil would get his due. That I had to find time for my own grieving."

He nodded but said nothing, clearly giving her space and time. She took both, but probably in a far larger way than he meant them. Because *this* was not the time either.

"Who's getting first watch?" she asked.

"I'll take it," he answered promptly. "I think your night last night was far more disturbed than mine."

So she pulled back the flap on the sleeping bag and lay down with her back to him, pulling the cover over herself, hunching her shoulder a little as if to hold him away.

No, she hadn't had much time for grief. But right now

she did, and for the first time in a long time, she let the tears fall silently. In a few hours, maybe in the morning, she could be strong again.

But right now she felt an overwhelming need to shed tears for her lost husband and her daughter.

If there was any sadness in this house, she thought, it only echoed her own.

During the night she awoke to feel strong arms around her, a strong body pressed to hers from behind. The feeling was at once startling and familiar. She felt Mike's warm breath near her ear, a steady sound as if he slept, too.

But weren't they supposed to remain awake to listen?

She didn't want him to roll away. No, she wanted him to stay right there. It had been so long since she'd felt this kind of comfort, and this was the second time in a single day that he'd managed to remind her just how much she missed it.

She tried to remain still, so as not to wake him, afraid the almost magical moment would end, proving that it really was an illusion. And it was. She knew that. But it was an illusion she wanted to cling to.

Her breathing must have changed.

"You were dreaming," he murmured near her ear. "It didn't sound happy. Sorry if I woke you."

She wasn't, but she couldn't say so. "I don't remember any dream."

"It didn't sound like one you'd want to remember. Go back to sleep."

"It must be my turn to keep watch."

"No. I'm not at all sleepy yet." A moment of silence, then, "I can move away."

"No. Please." So many empty, worried, frightened, lonely nights lay behind her. The last thing she wanted right now was to add yet another one.

He gave her a little squeeze and continued to hold her, almost as if he was feeling the same way: too many lonely nights haunted him.

What a pair, she thought. He was afraid of connections because life had taught him, probably more often than he had told her about, that he was unwelcome because of his heritage. And then there she was, afraid of the same thing, for probably the same reasons. Because if she were to be honest about it, the idea of putting her whole life on hold until Colleen grew up was kind of ridiculous. The only valid reason she could have for that kind of decision was fear that she might fall for someone who wasn't good for Colleen. Beyond that…

Beyond that she'd been hiding. Because she was afraid. Because her heart had been ripped out once, and she didn't want to risk it again.

At least, she told herself, *be honest about what you're doing.*

And much to her surprise, she heard herself say, before she was even aware of the thought, "Do you date?"

She thought she felt him stiffen a little, but she couldn't be certain. Then he said, "Not often."

"Me neither. I was just thinking that I'm afraid."

"Of dating?"

"Of caring."

"I can sure see why."

"Ditto."

"Ouch." But he said it without any real emphasis, as if he knew perfectly well that he was hiding from pain.

She gave him marks for that. "Unfortunately," she said quietly, "I think I've been making Colleen my excuse."

"How so?"

"Too busy. She needs me, and I can't divide my time that way. Oh, there's probably a whole list of reasons that are buried in my subconscious."

"Probably. That's only human."

"But for you it's different. Why don't you just go home and find some nice young woman who won't kick you and call you names?"

A long silence answered her.

"I'm sorry," she said presently. "None of my business."

"No, I was just thinking it over. The trouble is, I'm not sure why. Maybe because I worked so hard to get away, to walk into this world and be accepted, at least partly, for my skills. Maybe I ran away from the past."

"Another common human thing to do," she murmured. "We all have our ways of hiding."

"Too true." He was quiet for a while and shifted his hold on her, bringing her closer until the back of her head rested comfortably in the hollow of his shoulder. "I don't have a lot of people left at home that I would consider close. No real reason to go back. I did a pretty good job of separating myself. Maybe it was the stupidity of youth."

"I don't know that I would call it stupidity. A lot of us grow up wanting to escape whatever rut we think we're in."

"True. And we rebel against expectations, and

traditions. I don't know. I *do* know that when I go back to visit it feels like I have to look at the same old questions over and over again."

"Which questions?"

"About who I am. What I am. And how I fit."

Struggling against the confines of a sleeping bag that seemed to want to hold on to her like duct tape, she managed to turn over until they were face-to-face. She could barely make him out in the darkness, but she could see the glint of his eyes and the shape of his head. Even the suggestion of his mouth and nose.

"I can't imagine it," she said. And instinctively she reached up to brush her fingers against his cheek. "It would seem to me that you should fit anywhere you choose to. I guess that's where I have an advantage. No big deal that I didn't want to be a ranch wife. A much bigger deal for you not to stay within your culture and become what your uncle wanted."

"And that's just the beginning."

She turned that around in her mind as she waited for him to say more, but he remained silent. And then a thought occurred to her. "Do you feel *guilty* for leaving?"

"Just a bit."

"But why?"

He snorted quietly. "My ancestors didn't choose to abandon their culture or their way of life. It was forced on them. And those cultures are slowly but surely changing and evaporating. Well, maybe not so slowly. Remember, it hasn't been all that long. Three, maybe four generations for some of us. Less for others. So when I walked away, I put another nail in the coffin of my people's ways. So yeah, it makes me feel a bit guilty. The fire is dying. The light is going out. The bits that we've managed to cling to have for many become a tourist attraction, or a quaint mythology. Kids want to bust out of the limited opportunities on the rez. They want the whole oyster, just the way I did. Perfectly natural, I guess. Sadly, for native populations there are only two choices left—live the old ways and die out, or build a casino and live the antithesis of the old ways."

"I hadn't thought about it that way."

"No reason you would." He stirred a little as if resettling himself into a more comfortable position. "It's inevitable. Eventually we'll be little more than someone's record of us in an ethnography. Time marches on, things change, and the stories I was told while growing up will eventually be nothing but stories."

"But that's not a good thing, is it?"

"Of course not. Why else do I feel guilty? There are a lot of things well worth preserving in native cultures. Unfortunately, the world doesn't seem to work that way. The sands of time bury us all sooner or later."

"And you feel like one of those sands?"

"Sometimes."

"But not all the time?"

"No, not always. But I feel a pull, and one of these days I may do more than send donations. I may go back there to stay."

That frightened her a bit, though she wasn't sure why. "To do what?"

"Oh, I could teach. I could look after animals. There are lots of things that need doing. Always." He sighed quietly. "But the fact remains that while there are twelve thousand enrolled members of the Northern Cheyenne, fewer than five thousand remain on the reservation."

"So a lot of others have moved away, too?"

"Yup. A steady drain, until one day we're gone."

"That is so sad." When she thought of extinctions, she thought in terms of biological species, but he was talking about something very different. "You're watching an extinction," she whispered.

"Exactly. Slowly and steadily. And it'll take a lot more than me going back to stop it. Cheyenne blood will last a lot longer than Cheyenne culture."

She nodded against his shoulder, absorbing what he was saying and feeling a definite pang of sorrow.

"I guess," he said after a moment, "that we'll become museum curiosities, if we aren't already."

"That's awful!"

He surprised her with a quiet chuckle. "It's awful, but it's inevitable. Whatever we preserve will eventually survive only in museums. I suppose the good thing is that there's an effort under way to preserve it at all. And my people have been changing for a long time anyway."

"What do you mean?"

"We're Algonquian. We started out back east, moved to the upper Midwest, then continued our westward journey, most likely because of pressures coming from the East and all the Europeans. We were farmers, then we became Plains hunters. So we've been adapting all along. Who knows how much of our current culture was adopted along the way as we migrated."

"That's very philosophical."

"Show me a healthier way to look at it. Because I sure as hell can't stop it any more than you could return to a sod hut in the nineteenth century."

"So true. And that's where my ancestors, at least

in the local area, started. In a sod hut. It's still on the property, but now it looks more like a hill. When I was a kid, I tried to dig into it. You know, like an archeological site. I was sure stuff must have been left behind in there when the family finally moved into a house. My dad stopped me though."

"How come?"

"Because he was afraid there might still be hollows inside, and that it could collapse on me."

"So you became a renovator instead, still hunting for treasures."

She gave a short, soft laugh. "I guess so. In some ways it's not that different. I find treasures from time to time. Old postcards, an earring. Once I even found a locket."

"What did you do with them?"

"I keep them in a little box. Somehow I don't feel right about throwing them away. Maybe in some silly way I feel that someone someday might show up who would find meaning in them."

"That's an intriguing thought."

Then she heard him murmur a total non sequitur. "Tell me to stop."

Before her brain could even begin scrambling around to figure that out, his mouth met hers. At first the touch was tentative, as if he expected rejection, but rejection was the last thing in her heart or mind.

Every bit of awareness she'd tried to shove into her subconscious over the past couple of days leaped to the forefront of her mind and body. Instead of pulling away, instead of protesting as he wanted her to, she leaned into his kiss, seeking a much deeper connection.

Electricity sparked along her nerve endings. Synapses

long asleep awoke in a huge wave of hunger and desire.
Yearning filled her, yearning for a man's touches, and
man's possession. All the things she'd been without for
so long.

And perversely, the very caution in him that had tried
to warn her away now seemed like a promise of safety.
Whatever happened between them here and now would
not go any further. He would pull back to save himself,
and in so doing would save her *from* herself.

And that perverse sense of safety unleashed the
explosion of need. She leaned into him, against him,
twining her arm around his neck, wanting him closer,
needing him closer. Reveling in the feeling of a man's
hard body pressed tightly to hers, even through layers
of clothing and sleeping bag.

A quiet groan escaped him, she felt a shudder run
through him, and then he gave up the battle, just as she
had.

Right here, right now, all the barriers dissolved into a
more primitive force than culture or race. And all those
barriers had never seemed more irrelevant. They were
just imaginary, man-made boundaries to the elemental
need to mate, man and woman.

His kiss deepened as she welcomed him. She felt
his leg lift to drape heavily over hers. The sleeping
bag was between them, but at that moment it was the
only acknowledged barrier. Anything else had instantly
vaporized in the heat of longing.

God, she wanted him. Wanted this stolen night, these
explosive moments of passion. If there would be a price
later, she was past caring.

His hands worked their way inside her sleeping bag,
then up under her shirt until skin touched skin. The

sensation was electric, and so, so good. Her back seemed to come alive under his touch, more nerve endings awakening to the thrill of being alive.

And how long had it been since she had allowed herself to feel that?

Too long, because almost as soon as skin touched skin, she felt a deep, almost painful throb between her legs as her body took over.

Her brain became incapable of any thought except a yearning to be touched, *here,* or *there…* She nearly held her breath in anticipation, every ounce of her being focused on those fingers that stroked so lightly against her back, trespassing no farther although she wanted him to trespass everywhere.

She could feel the tension and heat building in him as well, could sense in the way his body tightened, in the pressure against her abdomen, and sensing his need inflamed her own.

She was wanted. God, it had been so long since she'd been wanted….

His hand slipped around, up under her bra, cupping her breast in heat. Desire zinged through her and she arched against his legs. Needing no more invitation, he caught her nipple between thumb and forefinger, brushing it, twisting it gently, sending more shock waves running throughout her body.

She ached. Oh, how she ached. She pressed herself harder into his hand, tried to bring her hips to meet his, felt the rocking response of his body against her. She managed to clutch his shoulder, telling him with her grip that she wanted it all, every bit of it, right now.

He groaned softly and deepened his kiss, now pushing his leg hard up between hers, pressing on her aching core, and it felt good, so good that she became instantly damp.

She burned for him, and somewhere deep inside, some part of her was holding its breath in anticipation, wishing away clothes, wishing away everything that separated them.

"Mike, please!" It was the only way she could tell him. A plea for more and yet more. He mumbled something she couldn't quite make out.

Then a loud bang sounded through the house.

At once they both froze. Mike swore, and before she could make a sound he had leaped to his feet. She struggled against the sleeping bag that seemed to have become the arms of an octopus, grabbing at her and refusing to free her.

Still struggling, she blinked as the camp lantern came on and she cried a protest as she saw he was about to leave the room.

"No, wait!"

He paused, looking back at her, his face cast into eerie shadows by the lantern he held low. "No, stay here," he said. "If someone's in the house…"

If someone's in the house? He'd spoken the words quietly, but they seemed to ring deafeningly in her head.

If someone was in the house, the last place she wanted to be was tangled up in a sleeping bag, alone.

By the time she got out of that damn sticky sleeping bag, Mike had vanished. She could tell where he had gone only by the dim glow from the lantern as he moved through the downstairs rooms.

By the time he reached the staircase, ready to ascend, she was there, determined to go with him. He looked at her, as if he wished she'd listened to him, but he didn't argue.

Together they climbed the stairs, with him just two risers ahead of her. She kept her feet to the outside of the risers, so as not to make them creak, and he did the same.

She was convinced, absolutely convinced, that someone had to be in the house. The windows weren't open so there was no way on earth the wind could have blown one of those doors shut.

And she was mad. Sexual arousal and adrenaline weren't far apart on the biological scale, at least to judge by what she felt. She was angry that someone might be trying to scare her, although she couldn't imagine why anyone would, and furious that those precious moments with Mike, that wonderful budding sense of being a woman again, had been truncated.

A switch had just been flipped, from her earlier concern that Colleen was uncomfortable to one of sheer fury. Whoever was responsible for this crap would pay.

Maybe she was forgetful. Maybe she laid down tools and other equipment in her preoccupation and forgot where she'd placed them. She could accept that explanation for things seeming to move around. She could even accept that vermin in the walls could make the noises that frightened Colleen. But a door slamming? Twice now?

Unless they found a window open, there could only be one explanation.

They got to the head of the stairs and Mike reached out, flipping on the lights. No more tiptoeing in the dark. Getting out of here now would involve someone rushing past them or scrambling out a window and over the front porch roof, any one of which would be a dead giveaway.

But nothing happened.

Room by room they walked through the upstairs and found nothing at all.

Del felt her lips tightening with anger. This could not continue. She would not allow this to continue.

Except she had no idea at all how to put an end to it.

Back downstairs, in silent agreement, they went to the kitchen. It was nearly 5:00 a.m. The sun would be coming up soon, and apparently the night was over, at least as far as sleeping went.

Still furious, Del went to put on a pot of coffee. Mike disappeared for a few moments and returned with a bag. He placed it on the counter and began pulling out an assortment of snack foods: chips, pretzels, even a tray of raspberry Danish from the local bakery. "What would you like?" he asked.

"Sugar. Energy."

"Danish it is." He ripped the plastic wrap off the aluminum tray and hunted up some small plates and a knife.

"That wasn't vermin," she said. She leaned against the counter, facing the coffeepot, her head resting against a cabinet.

"No," he agreed.

"And don't tell me the house is sending a message."

"Never crossed my mind."

But she sensed the stiffening in him, as if she had just insulted him. Damn it. Were they always going to have to tiptoe around sensibilities?

"Look," she said, "I didn't mean anything critical by that."

"No?" He sighed and put two plates of Danish on the table. "Maybe not."

"I didn't. But if I'm going to have to measure every word against some form of political correctness, we're going to spend a lot of time being angry."

"Or I could just leave."

"Oh, that'll solve a lot," she said, pivoting abruptly to face him. "Just walk away. That always clears the air."

"Del…"

But she interrupted him. Something had been building in her, some point of snapping rapidly approached. She didn't know why, unless the past four years were finally catching up with her, aggravated by sounds she couldn't explain, a frightened daughter and now a neighbor who, while he seemed to be trying to help her, had also added a whole additional area of concern.

"Look, I'm me, and you're you," she said. "We have different backgrounds. I don't have a particular problem with that, regardless of what you seem to think. And if I'm tired and a bit crabby and I say something not exactly right, I'd appreciate it if you would not put five hundred years of ugly history on *my* shoulders."

Silence hung so thickly in the room that she felt it nearly impossible to draw a breath. Mike didn't move a muscle. His face revealed not a single thing.

Well, she thought, that had blown it. Too little sleep, too much worry, noises she couldn't explain, and it had all come together to make her blow up like some fringe lunatic over absolutely nothing. She should apologize. If nothing else, she should at least apologize.

But then he astonished her by saying simply, "You're right."

She sucked a breath so deep it felt as if she must have stopped breathing throughout the silence as she waited for his reaction. "What?" Stupid question, but his words seemed out of sync with what was going on inside her.

"I said, you're right. I think of it as being smart and not getting involved in dangerous situations, but in point of fact I'm walking around with a bunker mentality, waiting for the next artillery round to land. And damn near everything hits me like an artillery shell. My own emotional version of shell shock."

"I'm sorry," she whispered, feeling more than anger now, something that overwhelmed anger completely. Whatever her problems, she could scarcely imagine the life experiences that had taught him this.

"You have nothing to apologize for." He passed his hand over his face before continuing. "You're right. I overreacted to something you said because you're upset and worried, and you have every right to be. And I've been muttering on about how this house feels sad— and I won't take that back because it *does*—so why wouldn't you expect me to say something like the house is slamming doors? It must all sound like mumbo jumbo to you."

"But that's the thing," she said with a surprising amount of vehemence, maybe bordering on a plea. "It *doesn't* sound like mumbo jumbo. It's just a different way of looking at things I've basically always believed! In my faith there are angels and saints, and even, if I'm willing to go that far, demons. If that's part of my belief system, then why not the things you said earlier? It even makes a kind of sense."

His eyebrows lifted, as if it surprised him that she should say such a thing. "What do you mean?"

"Well, like you said, if God created the universe, what did he create it out of? Why not awareness in rocks and trees? Different awareness, maybe, but why not? I'm having less trouble with that idea than you would think."

"Wow."

"Wow?"

"Wow." The faintest of smiles touched his lips. "Just don't go New Agey on me."

"I'm not sure New Age is all wet." She sighed. Her eyes felt as if they were full of sand, and her body just wanted to sag in the wake of her anger. "I mean, I don't buy most of it, but who am I to say it's totally wet? Why do you object to New Age?"

"Because they try to glom on to bits of my people's beliefs and twist them to their own purposes."

"Well, I'd resent that, too. I'm sorry I sniped at you, but I'm not going to accept the possibility that the door-slamming sound originated with anything except a human being."

"I agree. And that seriously concerns me. So before this day is over, we're going to move Colleen into my house with your aunt, or find some other suitable arrangement. And if you don't talk to the sheriff about this, I will."

At least it was a plan. It wouldn't solve the problem, but it would take the biggest worry off her plate: Colleen. Right now she wouldn't bring Colleen back into this house for any reason. She didn't want her daughter scared any more than she was already.

"I don't know about talking to the sheriff," she said. Behind her, the coffeepot popped and released a blast of steam, letting her know it had finished brewing. She pulled some mugs from the cupboard then carried them and the pot of coffee to the table.

Mike sat facing her as she poured coffee. "Why not go to the sheriff? Something's not right."

"Obviously. But what have I got? The sound of a slamming door? And maybe some forgetfulness about where I put things? What could the sheriff possibly do about any of that?"

"I guess you're right." But he didn't look happy about agreeing. "And Colleen?"

She looked up from the piece of Danish she was cutting with her fork. "I agree. She's not coming back into this house until I get to the bottom of this. She's been through enough. But how do I get to the bottom? What if it's just somebody playing a practical joke?"

"I doubt a practical joker would be running around at this hour of the morning."

"Me, too." And that sense of creepiness started to return.

"But that leaves us with the huge problem of why someone would be trying to scare you or your daughter."

She put her fork down, facing the horrible sense that reality was spinning out of her control and that for once she couldn't grab the reins and bring it back in line. "I don't think I've done anything to make anyone that mad. And I seriously doubt Colleen has either."

"I'd be shocked if either of you had. So it's got to be something about this house."

Back to the house again. But she was out of arguments. She couldn't put this down to forgetfulness, early onset senility, distraction or mice in the walls. It had gone well past that. Especially since Mike had heard the sound both times.

So she wasn't going crazy, Colleen wasn't going crazy, and the likelihood that someone was pulling a prank was minimal at best. Heck, it wasn't as if Colleen had even reached the age where she might have friends who wanted to wrap toilet paper on the trees out front. And making strange noises in a house in the predawn hours went well past that.

"Man," she whispered.

"Eat," Mike finally said. "The calories will help. When do you have to get Colleen?"

"I need to pick her up around six-thirty so I can bring her back here to shower and change before school."

"Okay. I have surgeries starting at seven, but I'll do what I can to finish out early today. Maybe cancel some appointments."

She lifted her eyes to him again. "Then what?" she asked. "Then what?"

"I don't know," he admitted. "But we've got to figure out something. And soon."

Chapter 8

Colleen was happy to see her, even though it meant another day of struggling through school. And Colleen did struggle. She didn't complain about it, but Del had heard from teachers how the other kids bumped her around because her wheelchair got in the way. The only thing that seemed to have improved over the past couple of years was that no one picked on her anymore for it. They just got impatient, and going down a crowded hallway could be a problem. When the school had decided that Colleen should change classes just before or after the other kids, she had objected, claiming that everyone would be mad at her for getting special privileges. So she struggled through crowded hallways surrounded by kids who sometimes seemed blind to the fact that there was a girl in a wheelchair among them.

Del didn't understand it, but since Colleen's accident she had noticed how often people treated the disabled poorly, getting impatient with their slowness or the obstruction they seemed to cause. And maybe worst of all, how the disabled became invisible to those rushing around them.

Unfortunately, she had to take Colleen home before school. Much as she didn't want her daughter in that house right now, she had to. Colleen needed a shower, and there was only one place she could get one, and only one person who could help her with it. She wouldn't embarrass Colleen any further by asking anyone else to help with dressing and undressing, maneuvering into the chair in the shower, or washing her.

Colleen had already suffered enough indignities for a lifetime, and to some extent had to suffer them each and every day at the hands of her own mother.

"You moved my room!"

No way to hide that.

"Only until we get rid of whatever's making the noises. You can tell me later where you want your posters and things."

"It's farther from the bathroom."

"I'm sorry."

Colleen was frowning, clearly unhappy that she hadn't been consulted, but when Del accompanied her through her torn-up room, the frown faded to be replaced by a giggle.

"What's so funny?" Del asked.

"You sure made a mess for one mouse."

If only it were just a mouse, Del thought, but she managed a passable laugh in return. "It was going to happen sooner or later. You've been through this enough times to know."

Colleen sighed. "Yeah. Someday maybe we can live in just one house for a long time?"

Del felt her heart squeeze. "All this moving bothers you?"

"A little." Then, as if catching herself, Colleen looked up at her. "It's okay. It's what we have to do, right?"

"Right." But was it? It had initially been necessary because she couldn't afford two mortgages, but now she was paying two anyway. And then she was always afraid to leave a house unoccupied for long while she was working on it because there were so many useful things to steal.

And maybe that was too paranoid?

Or maybe not. Hell. She could hear that slamming door echo in her mind as she helped Colleen bathe and dress for school.

And she decided not to tell Colleen that there was going to be another change that very afternoon. She'd do it later, when she picked her daughter up from school.

As she did every morning, she lifted Colleen into the passenger seat of her truck and put the wheelchair in back in the bed. As she did every morning, she reversed the process at school, then stood and watched as Colleen wheeled herself along the sidewalk, up the ramp and through a door that a teacher opened for her.

Her throat tightened. She squeezed her eyes shut and sent a message winging heavenward, about how unfair life had been to this little girl.

As soon as she did, she felt guilty for it. She'd seen kids in the hospital and in therapy who had it far worse. But sometimes trying to feel grateful that it wasn't worse felt damn near impossible.

Finally, as she heard the bell ring inside the building,

she climbed back into her truck and pulled out her cell phone. In just a short time, she heard Nate Tate's gravelly voice answer.

"Hi, Sheriff, it's Del Carmody."

"Del! Hot damn. You work so hard I never get to see you around. And what's with the sheriff thing? It's Nate to you now."

She felt a smile crease her face, and so many memories came flooding back. Just the sound of Nate's voice was comforting. She had a string of memories of all the times he came into her classroom, before he had retired and she had moved away, to talk about the law, about not being stupid behind the wheel, or just to give students a glimpse of how the sheriff's office worked, and what it was like to be a deputy.

And then there were the other times, good times. Nate had six daughters, and Del had gone through school with some of them. And that had meant pajama parties, and barbecues, and birthday bashes. There was a time when it hadn't been unusual to see twenty or even thirty girls crammed into the Tate house, all giggling and laughing. There had even been one memorable time when they'd camped in the backyard, trying without much success to keep the volume down so the neighbors wouldn't complain, only to be sent inside in a rush by an unexpected thunderstorm.

"How are you holding up?" Nate asked her now. "You ought to come by some time for coffee."

"Well, I was going to ask if I could do that sometime today. I'd like to pick your brain."

"Brain's always open for picking. If you're not busy right now, come on over. The coffee is fresh."

"Thank you. I'm on my way."

The Tates still lived on the edge of town, their ranch-style house set on a large lot surrounded by similar houses from the same era. Every so often, the town grew in a spurt. Del didn't know what spurt had caused this particular subdivision, as it had been here as long as she could remember. At the other end of town, the relatively new semiconductor plant had caused another spurt of growth: houses and apartments both.

Nate hadn't changed much in the course of the past twenty years or so, at least not to Del's eye. The man had always seemed ageless. And Marge, his wife, while a little plumper around the middle, showed her years only in the gray hair that had replaced her once-fiery mane. Both of them welcomed Del warmly, and soon she was on the sofa, holding a mug of coffee, with a plate of small pastries on the table at her elbow.

"How's Colleen doing?" Marge asked immediately.

"Surprisingly well," Del admitted. "I keep waiting for her to erupt one way or another, but she doesn't."

"Some people," Nate remarked, "roll more easily with the punches than most. Maybe she's been blessed that way."

"I hope so." And indeed Del did. Not a thing could be done about her daughter's paralysis, so the best she could hope for was that Colleen could remain upbeat and happy.

"So you wanted to pick my brain," Nate said presently, when the social niceties were out of the way. "What about?"

Del looked down into her mug, uncertain how to even begin. Sitting here in the Tate house, the whole thing sounded ridiculous even as she tried out words in her mind.

Finally Nate spoke again. "There isn't much I haven't heard, Del. Some of it far stranger than you could even imagine."

At that she looked at him and smiled. "I believe you. It's just… Oh, I don't know. I was going to ask you if anything had ever happened in that house I'm working on over on Jackson. Anything bad."

His face didn't reflect even a smidgen of surprise. Instead he asked, "What's going on?"

She sighed. "Nate, it sounds insane."

"A lot of things do. So just tell me what's going on. The best place to start is usually the beginning."

"Well, it started with Colleen hearing noises in her room. I thought we had mice or something, and for a week or so I tried to ignore it, thinking they'd go away as I continued pulling down walls. I looked around, of course, but couldn't even find any sign that something had been in the attic. And Colleen was getting frightened."

Nate nodded encouragingly and Marge left her bentwood rocker to come sit beside her and pat her hand comfortingly.

"Anyway," Del continued, "Colleen went to spend the night with a friend on Saturday, so I decided to sleep in her room and see if I could identify the noises. I heard it. And I don't mind telling you, it scared me, too. So much so I ran out of the house and didn't want to go back in. Mike Windwalker saw me outside on the porch and came over to see what was wrong. He sat in Colleen's room, too, and heard the same thing. Crazy as it may be, it absolutely did *not* sound like animal scratching. It sounds…well, it sounds almost like human fingers. Soft, not like claws."

"Okay," Nate said. "I don't think you're crazy. What happened next?"

"Mike and I spent all Saturday ripping out the plaster in Colleen's room until I could pull enough lath loose to look in the walls. I couldn't find any sign that animals had ever been in there. And by then we'd heard some other noises, too."

"Like what?"

"Doors slamming. Heavy doors. Except none of the doors in the house had slammed. And when we made them slam, we realized it shook the house. We could feel the vibrations when we did it, but none when we just heard it."

Marge squeezed her hand, and Nate frowned faintly.

"That's strange all right. Anything else?"

"Just that I seem to keep misplacing things. I'm probably just not being as attentive as usual what with Colleen being scared."

"Could be." Nate's eyes remained both kind and thoughtful as he looked at her. "What aren't you telling me?"

Del almost jerked backward in surprise. No wonder this man had been such a good sheriff. How could he guess there was more? She hesitated, because she didn't know how Mike would feel about her spreading this.

"You can't tell anyone else," she said finally.

"I won't." Nate smiled. "I've been keeping this county's secrets most of my adult life. So has Marge."

"I'll leave if you want," Marge said gently.

"No, no, it's just that I don't think this is the type of thing Mike would want getting around."

"It won't," Nate promised.

"He says the house feels sad." She felt her own jaw thrust forward, almost belligerently, because if he said one thing critical about Mike she was going to…going to what? Nate wouldn't do that. He'd been the man to hire the county's first two Native American deputies.

He asked, "And that's why you wanted to know if something bad had happened in the house?"

"Basically. Or anything else. I mean, right now we're both pretty convinced that someone is trying to scare me, but we can't figure out why. And we thought maybe if we looked into the house's history, we might get a clue. Obviously the place was built by someone with money. Could someone think there's some kind of treasure in there?"

"I've never heard even a rumor like that." He sat back and rubbed his chin, obviously ruminating. "Something in the house that someone wants to find first? Possible. Some reason someone wants to scare you out? Equally possible. Or some just plain mean person wants to make your life more difficult? Much as I hate to admit it, I've known people like that. Somebody might have taken some wild notion about you or even your daughter. Some folks are that low. Someone might even object to the noise of your renovations and be too mealymouthed to just come out and tell you."

Del nodded slowly. "I hadn't even thought about that. I asked my neighbors to let me know if I disturb them, but so far no one's said anything."

"Hmm." Nate fell silent for a few minutes. "Well, that's one hell of a hodgepodge of things. Can't even be sure all of them are related."

"I know. I feel silly for even troubling you with it."

At that Nate smiled. "If I didn't like folks troubling

me with things, I wouldn't have stayed sheriff for so long. Marge'll tell you."

"I certainly will." Marge smiled warmly. "And lately, he's been getting a bit cranky because he misses the action. So you see? Coming here was a good thing to do."

"I'm not getting cranky," Nate protested mildly, but he winked at Marge as he said it. "I'm going to need to think this over, Del. Something's obviously going on. These occurrences happen at any particular time?"

"Mostly in the evening or during the night, but we did hear a door slam in the afternoon. And we couldn't find a thing."

Nate nodded. "As for Mike saying the house is sad…well, he may be right. I'm the last one to question that kind of intuition. But what would leave that impression?"

Marge shook her head. "I don't remember anything unusual connected to the house. I seem to remember Barb Barrow died there, but she was old and that was nearly forty years ago, wasn't it?"

"That's right. They found her in bed. Looked like a peaceful passing and she was ninety-five. Hardly enough to make a house sad."

Del was surprised that Nate didn't seem to have a problem with the idea that Mike thought the house was sad. Quite the contrary, he seemed to consider it an important clue. She had expected skepticism, although no bigoted comments, not from Nate Tate.

"I've got to give this some thought," Nate said after a moment. "As far as I know, nothing unusual has ever happened there."

Marge spoke. "Barb Barrow was fairly well-to-do. Didn't she and her husband build the place?"

"I think so." Nate's gaze grew distant with thought. "But she wasn't batty. I vaguely remember the probate proceedings. There was enough money in her bank account that I doubt she left any in the walls or under floorboards. It wasn't like any of her heirs claimed there was missing jewelry or something. Besides, this is an awfully late date for someone to want to hunt for valuables like that."

"Maybe," Del said, "I should check the newspaper morgue."

"Easier to go to the library," Nate said. "Miss Emma will have everything at her fingertips. Meantime I'll talk to a few people, put the old ear to the ground."

When she left a half hour later, Del felt considerably better. Why? She didn't know, except Nate Tate had a way of making people feel more relaxed, as if he'd somehow take care of things. And maybe he would. If one of her neighbors was mad about noise or something, Nate would surely be able to find out.

Although the idea of any of her neighbors running around in the middle of the night trying to scare her seemed ridiculous beyond belief.

In fact, the whole situation seemed ridiculous. Standing in the bright morning sunlight outside the library, in a world washed clean by the heavy rains, she would have found it easy to believe she had imagined everything. All of it. Except Mike had heard it, too. And Colleen.

And Colleen was scared.

The house was sad.

If she allowed even the possibility that the animism

with which Mike had been raised had even one iota of reality to it, then the house could be sad. And if the house was sad...

Squaring her shoulders, she marched into the library. Miss Emma, as she was known to everyone, sat at her small desk behind the circular wooden counter. She looked up and greeted Del with a smile. "Well, it's been a while," she commented as she rose to greet Del. "I thought you were too busy to read."

"Unfortunately, I usually am. But that's not why I'm here. Nate suggested you might be able to help me out. I need to know if anything bad ever happened in the house I'm working on now."

Emma's green eyes narrowed thoughtfully. "The old Barrow place, right?"

Forty years since elderly Mrs. Barrow had died, and yet the place would probably forever be *the old Barrow place*. That was one of the things Del loved about living here. "That's it."

"I don't recall anything offhand, but I can look. I helped the editor get most of the newspaper morgue onto microfiche and indexed on the computer."

"That must have been some job."

Emma laughed. "I'm always coming up with ideas like that. These days librarians are seldom overworked. Between TV and paperback books, most people show up here only when they need to do some serious research. The more databases I can develop, the busier I keep myself."

"Well, now that's a comment on modern life."

Emma, still smiling, shrugged. "It's easier for most people to click something online and have it delivered to their doors. But for research, there's nothing like your local librarian. Tell you what, it'll give me something to do today, and I'd probably be faster than you at working my way through the database, so why don't I research the address for you? I'll call later, whether I find anything or not."

"That would be wonderful!"

"I'd actually enjoy it. And I've been working on putting together a really detailed history of this county, so who knows? Maybe I'll find a good story to add to my book."

Which left Del standing on the street at nine-thirty in the morning and few choices. She knew she should go back to the house and work. She shouldn't allow a few noises to scare her off. At the very least she could wedge doors open so she could be absolutely certain they weren't slamming around. Maybe if she kept looking she'd find something in the walls, like a raccoon. Something big. Something she'd later laugh about and wonder how she could have missed it.

At least that was how she tried to buck herself up.

But it didn't prevent her from making a stop at the hardware store first. Once there she bought some new window latches. Maybe she ought to consider having the locksmith come out to rekey the locks on the doors. No need to replace them when the current door locks were reasonably new and could be rekeyed.

Feeling a bit better, she drove home, her first task to check every window latch in the house.

Pulling into the driveway, though, she felt a prickle of apprehension, which she hadn't felt even a few days ago. Sunny skies, beautiful weather, and she sat in her truck feeling as if severe storm clouds were gathering around that house.

No, she definitely wasn't bringing Colleen back into that house unless she got to the bottom of these noises.

Sighing, she grabbed the bag from the hardware store and let herself into a house she had once loved and now was coming to hate.

Ridiculous, she told herself. *You're being ridiculous.* The house couldn't do anything to her, even if *was* sad. She knew that.

Stepping through the door, however, felt like stepping into another universe. Even the sun spilling through so many windows, brightening the dusty wood floors, shining off walls and paint, couldn't make her feel comfortable.

Window latches. All of a sudden, she decided she wasn't going to be cheap about it. Every window would get a new latch, no matter how good the old one might seem. And if that meant another trip to the hardware store, so be it.

Before she started her task, however, she called her aunt Sally and made sure the woman wouldn't mind watching Colleen at Mike Windwalker's place. Of course Sally didn't mind. There was a time when the woman would have insisted on bringing Colleen to her place, but Sally was no longer as steady, strong or nimble has she had been just a few years ago. The idea of staying at Mike's house seemed actually to appeal to her.

That taken care of, Del went to work. She needed a screwdriver and a chisel, and she stuck a rubber hammer in her tool belt. Some of those latches had been painted around so many times over the years, she was sure they were probably stuck to the wood beneath.

Because of the latch she had found open on Friday,

she decided to start in the kitchen. There were a great many windows, a lot of them big enough for a grown man to crawl through easily. The current locks could be jimmied open from the outside with a chisel, but the new ones wouldn't allow that.

When she finished in the kitchen, she was startled to see that it was already two-thirty in the afternoon. Time to wash up a bit and go get Colleen and then Sally.

At least she hadn't heard any noises.

Sighing, she wiped perspiration from her forehead with her sleeve then went to the sink for a quick scrub down. No time for a shower.

Colleen was already waiting in her chair on the sidewalk when Del pulled up. She looked so tired that Del felt her heart squeeze as she climbed out of the truck.

As soon as she reached Colleen, she squatted in front of her daughter so they were nearly at eye level. "You okay, sweetie?"

"Yeah."

"But you don't look like it."

Colleen gave her a moment of panic by looking away and biting her lip. Slowly her green eyes tracked back.

"What is it?" Del prompted gently.

"I don't want to go home," Colleen admitted in a muffled voice.

"Why not?"

Colleen hesitated again, then finally blurted, "Those noises. I hate those noises. And I'm tired of pretending they're just a mouse."

Del's heart skipped a beat and she sat back a little, balancing more on her heels. "Want to talk about it here or in the truck?"

"But I don't want to go home!"

Del sighed. "You're not going home. Not for long anyway."

"What do you mean?"

"We're going to get Aunt Sally, and then the two of you are going to stay at Mike's house until he and I get rid of the noises."

Colleen frowned. "You're not kidding me?"

"About something this important? Do you think I would?"

Slowly Colleen shook her head, and her shoulders relaxed a bit. "No, but…"

"But what?"

"We have to live in that house. What if you don't get rid of the noises?"

"Then we'll go back to the other house."

"Promise?"

"Promise." If for no other reason than Colleen had enough on her plate, and Del could no longer believe it was just a mouse. Putting Colleen back in that house before the problem was solved would be utter cruelty. "Have you been worrying about this all day?"

Colleen gave a reluctant nod.

"Why didn't you tell me just how much the noise was disturbing you?"

"Because I don't wanna be a wuss. Because you need for us to live in the house you're fixing."

Those words nearly broke Del's heart. How much pressure had she been putting on this child without realizing it? "What I don't need is for you to be miserable and scared. Stop trying to be strong for me, sweetie."

"Why? You're always strong for me."

Oh, crap. Del looked down at her knees, not knowing

what to say. Had she been too strong? If so, it had all been veneer. Had she set a bad example? Thrust too much on this child's shoulders by always trying to be upbeat and positive about every damn thing?

Dropping her knees to the pavement, she leaned forward and wrapped her arms around Colleen, hugging her tight. "I'm sorry," she whispered. "I thought I was doing the right thing for you. But it's the wrong thing if you feel you have to hide your fears and pains from me."

Colleen answered with a hug. "Sometimes I'm so scared, Mommy. So scared."

Del's eyes burned, and tears started to run down her cheeks. "Me, too, sweetie. Me, too."

Del waited for the tears to pass and for Colleen's hold on her to loosen. By then the buses were gone and the schoolyard nearly empty. Only then did she lift her daughter and the chair into her truck and set out for Sally's house.

"Okay," Del announced as they rolled slowly down the residential street, "we start a new policy of honesty today."

"What's that?"

"I'm not going to pretend to be strong when I'm not feeling that way."

Colleen's answer was slow in coming. "Do you know how not to be strong?"

"Yeah. I've just been hiding it. From you, from me, from everyone."

"So you weren't kidding when you said you get scared?"

"I get scared all the time. I've just been keeping it to myself."

"What scares you?"

"That you might not be happy. That your daddy's gone. That there are noises in the house and I don't know why."

Colleen remained silent as they drove past rows of houses, until finally she blurted, "It seems like you always smile. Like no matter what happens you find a way to make it sound better."

"There's nothing better about some of the things that have happened to us, Colleen. Nothing better about them. And I guess I should have admitted that to you."

Colleen thought that over. "Okay. I know I'm still a kid, but I'm not little like I was when the accident happened. You don't have to pretend that everything is always okay."

Del felt a renewed ache. "I'm sorry. I thought I was making things easier for you."

"I know." Another pause. "Daddy's dead, Mom. Sometimes I have a hard time remembering him. But you remember him, don't you?"

"Yes. Yes, I do." Her voice broke and she didn't try to conceal it.

"So that has to be harder for you than for me. I'm lucky because I don't even remember the accident."

"I'm glad."

"And I'm paralyzed."

"Yes." Now Del's throat was almost too tight to speak.

"So if it's okay, I'd like to be sad about that sometimes."

"Of course it's okay!"

"I didn't want to upset you."

If she hadn't been driving, Del would have closed

her eyes with the pain. "I'm sorry. I made you feel that way, didn't I? Of course you're allowed to be sad about it. Mad about it. Whatever you need to feel."

"Mom?"

"Yes."

"Most of the time I don't think about it too much. You know?"

"I know."

"But sometimes I get really sad about it. Just so you know."

"I've been a little worried that you haven't gotten mad or sad since the first couple of months."

"Well, I kinda realized that we'd *both* lost Daddy, and I figured, well…it seemed wrong to make you hurt more."

Del hit the brakes and pulled over to the side of the street. As soon as she put the truck in Park, she reached over and hugged Colleen as tightly as she could.

"It's okay, Mom," said an extraordinarily wise thirteen-year-old. "We were just trying to take care of each other."

"Yes." She could taste her own salty tears. "I'm sorry. I was trying to do everything right, and I guess I did everything wrong."

"Nah." Colleen almost seemed to brush it off, but she gave her mother another tight hug. "Don't we have to get Aunt Sally? And I really get to stay at Mike's place tonight?"

"For as long as it takes me to figure out what's wrong with that house. And if I can't figure out what's wrong, I swear we're moving."

"Good deal," Colleen said as they separated. "I can live with that."

Del was sure her eyes were still red when they picked up Sally, who managed to squeeze onto the bench seat with Colleen in the middle. And Sally's mind was elsewhere.

"So Collie and I are spending the night at the vet's house, eh?"

Oh, man, Del thought as she heard her aunt's suggestive tone. She was already going through a wringer because of her conversation with Colleen, and now her aunt was going off the deep end? "Aunt Sally…"

"Don't bug Mom," Colleen said. "I just gave her a hard time."

"Well, he's such a handsome man. I keep wondering why he doesn't date."

"Because of nosy people like you," Del blurted in sudden annoyance. And she was happy, so happy, to hear Colleen giggle.

"What did I say?" Sally asked.

"He's just helping Mom find out what's wrong with the house. Right, Mom?"

But this time there was a certain knowingness to Colleen's tone. Del fought an urge to beat her head on the steering wheel. "I hardly know him," she said finally.

"That's the most interesting type," Sally remarked.

And Colleen giggled again.

Del took what comfort she could from the fact that the tense moments were past now. Sally dropped the subject of Mike, and Colleen seemed content now that she knew she didn't have to go back into that house until the problem was solved.

And she was utterly amazed to see Mike's van in

his driveway when she pulled into hers. He came out before she could even finish parking and crossed the lawn smiling.

A cautious smile, maybe because of Sally, but a welcoming one however restrained.

Del hopped out of the truck and hurried to greet him. "I didn't expect you home already."

"I told you I'd shorten my day somehow. All that was left was some routine checkups and vaccinations, easy enough to postpone." He went to help Sally out of the truck while Del pulled the wheelchair out of the truck bed.

"We've met," he said to Sally.

"Yeah, you took care of my cat until she died last year," Sally said. "I'm starting to think about getting another."

"I have a couple dozen you can choose from."

Sally rolled her eyes as Del unfolded and locked the wheelchair. "Darn cats breed like rabbits."

"Seems like it sometimes."

And then as easily as if he did it every day, Mike reached into the truck and scooped Colleen up in his arms.

"Okay?" he asked her.

She grinned. "More than okay. You're cooler than Mom."

"No way," he protested, a laugh in his voice.

"Moms aren't allowed to be cool," Colleen said. "It's some kind of law."

He settled her in her chair then let her arrange herself. Apparently, Del thought, he'd noticed more about how to handle Colleen than she would have guessed. Colleen insisted on doing as much as she could for herself, and had gotten quite good about adjusting her position in the chair and putting her legs where she wanted them.

She looked up at Mike with a grin. "So I'm staying at your place?"

"You bet. And I got it all ready for you and your aunt."

"Awesome! What did you do?"

Mike's smile broadened. "Come on over and I'll show you."

So Colleen wheeled down the driveway to the sidewalk and then up Mike's drive. No ramp to the porch, of course, so Mike gripped the handles on her chair and pulled her up backward while Del steadied her aunt by tucking her arm through hers.

Inside, the living room looked as if a genie had visited. A stack of brand-new videos rested on the player, and he'd even rolled up his area rugs so Colleen could move freely. There were also some new teen novels by the sofa, which had been made up like a bed, and a couple of teen magazines.

"This so looks like a pajama party," Colleen announced, smiling.

"That was the idea. Your aunt Sally can sleep in my bedroom. I even cleaned it all up for her. Fresher than a hotel room."

Del followed him as he showed Sally and Colleen through the house, but there was one problem: the bathroom. Then she saw the safety bar leaning in one corner in an unopened package.

"Oh, Mike," she said softly, as Colleen and Sally looked around in the kitchen.

He followed her stare. "Essential," he said with a

shrug. "But I wanted you to help me put it up because I don't want to make a mistake. Too dangerous."

"That is so, so kind of you. I was wondering how we'd do this part."

"I do think of some things. The shower...well, you have a seat for that, right? We can move that over here?"

"No problem at all." She already liked this man, but now her heart seemed about ready to burst. He'd thought of everything, and all without being asked.

"You'll tell me what else I need to do? I want Colleen to feel as comfortable and independent as I can possibly make her here. I would have hung a bar over the couch, but I don't know where to find one."

Her heart swelled even more. "We can bring over the one from my house. Obviously she won't be needing it there until we get this problem solved. Mike? You're really thoughtful."

She almost thought his cheeks colored. Hard to tell with the coppery tone of his skin, though.

"Nah. These are minimal things. Just let me know if you notice something else."

She went back to her house to get her toolbox to install the safety bar, and Mike accompanied her. With that simple act, he both reminded her of the threat that now seemed to lurk within her house, and the fact that she didn't have to face it alone.

By the time they got back to Mike's house, Sally and Colleen had begun to bake chocolate chip cookies in Mike's kitchen. Somehow she suspected the ingredients hadn't just been lying around.

Sheesh, this was turning into a day for throat-tightening emotions. First over her conversation with

Colleen, and then over Mike's obvious concern for her daughter.

While she and Mike worked on installing the bar, she turned over her talk with Colleen in her mind. The worst of it, she supposed, was that she'd set a bottled-up example that wasn't good for a child Colleen's age. Why hadn't Colleen had the anticipated reactions, the *normal* reaction to what she'd lost? Because her mother had bottled her own away, as if one mustn't do that.

Damn. She gave a screw an especially hard twist, then jerked in surprise when Mike's hand touched hers. "What's going on?" he asked.

"Later." She jerked her head toward the kitchen, to indicate Colleen and Sally. They at least gave her an excuse. She didn't know if she wanted to discuss any of this with anyone else yet. If ever.

Fact was, she'd gotten used to not discussing anything emotional with anyone.

She swore softly as she drilled in the last screw. Then she straightened and tested the bar with her full weight. Yup, it was good.

She packed her tools away then went to the hall and called toward the kitchen. "I have to go back to the house to get Colleen's clothes and a few other things. I also need to do some work. Is that okay?"

"Go!" Colleen called back. "You don't want to see me eat cookie dough."

"Probably not, so I'll pretend I didn't hear that."

"Good."

Mike accompanied her again. Once they were outside, he asked, "Did I do a bad thing by getting the stuff to make cookies? I know you said you have to watch what Colleen eats."

She managed a smile for him. "Once isn't a catastrophe. Right now I want her to have fun, sneak more cookies than she should, and just plain enjoy herself."

He walked silently beside her until they reached her front door. Finally he asked, "Did something happen?"

She hesitated as she unlocked the door. Should she tell him? "Oh, why not?" she asked herself, almost under her breath. Her insides felt as if they'd been tossed into a dryer and tumbled until up felt like down. "I guess I've been a bad mother."

"In what way?"

They stepped into the foyer and she closed the door, shutting out the world. Shutting in whatever was going on in this house. For some reason, she had to suppress an inexplicable shudder.

"Colleen and I had a talk," she said finally. She couldn't even look at him. "It seems I've been too strong."

"In what way?"

"I've been so busy trying to pretend everything is okay for Colleen's sake, that she felt obliged to do the same for me. Today she called me on it."

"Ouch."

She looked at him then. "Ouch?"

"Yeah." He shook his head just a bit. "Here you've been trying to do the right thing, be strong, hold it all together, and now you feel guilty for it. That's an ouch."

"Yeah. It is." She sighed. "I need to gather up her clothes. I need to bring the shower chair over. God knows how long it's going to take to get to the root of all of this. Emma's looking at the library for information on the house. I'm replacing all the window latches, and so far I've only gotten to the kitchen windows. I'd like to get that done today."

"I'll help in every way I can. But first?"

She finally looked at him. Before she could ask, he opened his arms and drew her into a snug hug. "I think a bit of this is in order," he said huskily.

Any urge to resist, to remain in her personal pond of private misery, evaporated as his arms closed around her. How could she have forgotten how good a hug could feel, or how much she could need one?

"I don't know what's wrong with me," she said against his shoulder, then drew in his wonderful scent, a scent that had become so pleasingly familiar just last night. He smelled so good...

"Want me to guess?"

"Sure, why not."

"How about that you've spent the past few years doing everything in your power to protect your daughter, and now something is going on in your home and you don't know how to protect her. You don't know what to do, and you feel like you're floundering for a solution."

She thought about that, then leaned in even closer. "You're good. That's probably at least part of it."

"Well, the other part might be that you've been fighting all these battles for a long time, pretty much by yourself. Even strong people can't always go it alone."

"Isn't that what you're doing?"

"I haven't had the kind of load you've been carrying."

"But you're all alone."

"Yeah. I'm alone. I go to work and I avoid other possible complications. Life simplified to a ridiculous point, I guess. You've got considerably more on your plate. You can't just go to work, come home and shut the world out."

She looked up at him, suddenly realizing something. "We're peas in a pod. We just have different ways of hiding."

"Apparently so. And I'm beginning to wonder if I'm ever going to outgrow that eighteen-year-old kid."

"Maybe you already have." She hugged him back, smiling wanly. "You're all mixed up in *my* life now."

"Yeah. And I'm not regretting it. It's funny, but when I decided to move back here, rather than start a practice out east, I told myself I was going to face down all those old demons. Then all I did was avoid them."

"I don't think you entirely avoided them."

"What do you mean?"

"You put yourself in a very public position here. It's not exactly the same as hiding in a cave."

"True, but I've avoided other stuff." His dark eyes were tight around the corners, but the tightness began to ease. For a moment, he looked about ready to say something else, but then he cocked his head and looked past her.

"Come on," he said suddenly, letting go of her. "Let's get Colleen's stuff together. We've got work to do."

She caught his arm, surprised by the sudden change in him. "Mike?"

He shook his head, but said with urgency, "Just a feeling. Let's just get going. *Now.*"

Chapter 9

Mike's urgency propelled Del despite the fact that a couple of disturbed nights and some heavy work over the past few days had left her tired. Normally at this time of day she'd be wrapping up, getting ready to make dinner and settle in for a restful evening.

Instead, after carrying the necessary items over to Mike's for Colleen, she and Mike worked their way through the house, changing locks on windows. Darkness was falling by the time they reached the last room, her bedroom. Del took a minute to pull out her cell phone and call Colleen. Everything was fine, she was assured, and then Sally got on the line to ask when the two of them were coming over, as she'd roasted a chicken and it was about to come out of the oven.

"Thanks, Sally. I want to change one last lock, then we'll come over."

"Just make sure you don't take so long that it's all cold."

"I won't. Promise. It's just one lock."

The window in her bedroom was a tall one, overlooking the backyard. She could reach the lock easily enough to simply turn it, but she needed more leverage and a closer position to wield a screwdriver, so she knelt on the broad window ledge.

The next thing she knew she lay on the floor on her back, looking up at Mike, who kneeled beside her.

"Don't move," he said, and he started to feel her arms and legs as if checking for broken bones.

"I didn't know you did people, too."

"There are times I'd prefer a fellow vet to some of the medical doctors I've seen."

"What happened?"

"The window ledge popped off and you took quite a spill. You hit your head on the bed frame, but you were out only a few seconds. Are there two of me?"

"I wish. Two of you would be wonderful. But no, you're still a singleton, and it's Monday, and I'm okay."

He started to smile. "The old brain and mouth are working great."

His touch was purely professional, but she could not help but be aware of his hands moving along her limbs. With every touch, a small campfire seemed to ignite. Great timing.

"I don't think anything's broken," he said presently. "Now try to move your toes and fingers."

They all wiggled obediently. "Everything's fine."

"Okay. Then let me help you sit up slowly."

As he put his arm behind her shoulders and started to lift her to a sitting position, he said, "Let me know if your neck hurts. Even a small twinge."

"Nothing," she told him when she reached a sitting position. Then she raised an arm to feel the back of her head. There was an ache there, but she'd felt worse. "Goose egg tomorrow."

"You'll probably be sore in more places than that."

"I can deal with that. I just need to get that lock changed."

"I can probably manage that. I'm not totally useless, you know."

She looked at him. "Am I doing it again?"

"Doing what again?"

"Trying to accomplish everything by myself when other people want to help? Trying to be superwoman when it's not even good for my kid?"

"I dunno. Are you?" There was a twinkle in his eye. "Come on, you can supervise, but I'm taller and in my humble veterinarian opinion, you just lost your leverage when that shelf popped off."

"I can't argue with that."

He held her elbow to steady her as she rose to her feet. "It's okay," she said when she was standing. "The room isn't spinning or tilting. You can take off your vet hat now."

"Good. Now I can play at your job."

A couple of steps took them back to the window. The ledge, about eight inches wide as was common in many older homes, had indeed popped off. In fact, it had cracked right where it ran under the window.

And what Del saw when she looked down made her gasp. "There's a book in there!"

Bending, she lifted the slim volume and used her sleeve to wipe the dust from it.

"Why would someone hide a book?" Mike asked.

"I don't know. Unless..." She opened the cover carefully and looked at the fly leaf.

It was stamped with a gold *Journal,* and beneath that was a handwritten name: Madeline James.

"Oh, it's someone's diary."

"Fantastic!" Mike leaned closer and looked over her shoulder. "Imagine some teenager finding a place like that to hide her diary from her parents."

"Yeah. And imagine her forgetting it was there." Del had to smile. "Colleen would think of something like that in her more impish moments."

"I have no trouble believing it."

She looked at him. "Let's take a look at it after we finish the lock."

"After dinner," he reminded her. "I gather Sally wants us over there soon."

"True." She tossed the diary on the bed. "I don't think Madeline James would mind us looking at it after all this time. Besides, I don't even know who she is."

They went to work and finished the new latch in just about ten minutes. Satisfied that now no window in the house could be jimmied, she and Mike collected her tools and the diary and headed downstairs.

Mike watched as she put the tools away. "You're compulsive about that, aren't you?"

"Putting my tools away? You bet. There's nothing

worse than knowing you have a screwdriver and not being able to find it."

"So that makes it even weirder that stuff is being moved around."

"Yup." She locked the box and stood. "Except it *is* possible that I get slack about it sometimes."

"I doubt it." He compressed his lips. "I was just thinking."

"Yes?"

"Everything has a place at my clinic. Everything. I know where every damn piece should be, whether it's in a drawer, in the sterilizer, whatever. I never have to look around wondering where I left something. That kind of practice is essential, and objects disappear only when someone else moves them. Every time I get a new assistant for example, we have to go through the 'everything has a place and everything in its place' routine. And for a week or so, things will disappear."

She nodded. "What are you driving at?"

"That once you've formed habits like that, you don't break them unless something major distracts you. I don't think you've been getting careless. So you know what?"

"What?"

"We're coming right back here after dinner. And we're going to keep watch again."

"That was my plan." She sighed and brushed her hands against her jeans. "Miss Emma hasn't called, so I guess she hasn't found anything out about the house yet, one way or another."

"What did Nate say?"

"He's putting his ear to the ground."

"I hear he has fantastic hearing. Wish I knew him better."

"Maybe we can remedy that after we solve our mystery. I should have him and Marge over for dinner." Then, looking around the mess that was the house, she gave a laugh. "Well, maybe after I get things in shape."

"Feel free to use my place."

They locked up then crossed the yard to his house. Del felt a pang when she saw all the light pouring out of his windows, an inviting sight. Then she remembered that since she'd moved in next door, she'd rarely seen more than a single light burning in one of his windows.

Loneliness and solitude stank.

They ate in the large kitchen, the four of them gathered around a nice dinette. Sally had apparently decided to pull out all the stops: roasted chicken, mixed vegetables and mashed potatoes with gravy.

Colleen seemed to be in much better spirits, probably owing to the fact that she didn't need to spend the night at home with the noises. And maybe an unusual amount of sugar from cookies had added to it.

She chattered cheerfully about her weekend with Mary Jo, talking about musical groups Del had never heard of, about movies Del had never seen, and boys.

Boys?

Del zeroed in, listening more intently. She had known that would happen eventually but...but... Not only was Colleen so young, but she was also paralyzed, and Del lived in fear of the slights and disappointments that would come her daughter's way over the next few years.

But at the moment, Colleen's interest seemed to be more general than specific, so maybe they could avoid the inevitable pain for a while longer.

Mike raved so much about the dinner that Sally began to blush and offer to cook for him anytime. Afterward Sally insisted on doing the dishes, so Del and Mike took the time to hang Colleen's trapeze bar over the couch and watch her try it out. She settled onto the couch with a big smile and a happy sigh.

"Have you decided on a movie yet?" Mike asked her.

As soon as they had a movie running and the DVD player remote in Colleen's hand, they headed back to Del's house with the diary. For some reason she'd been unwilling to leave it behind when they went for dinner, and now it seemed to be almost burning her hand.

They made a pot of coffee then sat at the kitchen table.

Del passed her palm over the cover of the diary, feeling its nubbed leather surface. "This feels like an invasion."

"Well, we can just skip here and there. It's not like we have to read the whole thing."

"True." She looked from the journal to him. "It's probably nothing but a lot of teenage angst and dreams."

He hesitated, then said, "I think it's more."

"A feeling?"

"Yeah. Like the house."

She realized she was having a similar feeling, and that it was holding her back from opening the book. "Mike?"

"Yes?"

"I'm getting a bad feeling about this."

"I know. I am, too."

"I'm not a fanciful person."

He looked straight at her. "And you think I am?"

"No, that's not what I meant. Maybe you're accustomed to getting these feelings. I'm not. That's all I meant. So when I get a feeling like this…" She hesitated. "Can I tell you something?"

"Of course."

"The day that Don and Colleen went skiing…all day long I had this feeling that something terrible was going to happen. I couldn't shake it. I tried to tell myself I was imagining it, made myself focus on work. I don't get these feelings. But that evening when the officers showed up at the house…" She shook her head, unable to continue.

"You weren't surprised," he said.

"No. It was almost as if at some level I'd been getting ready for it all day. As soon as I heard the bell ring, I knew what it was. Even though it could have been any one of my neighbors or friends."

A tear escaped, rolling down her cheek. She dashed it away impatiently. "God, I seem to be crying all the time lately."

"Maybe you have some catching up to do."

Maybe she did. She sniffled, blinking away one more stray tear, then drew a deep breath. "Let's do this."

The cover made a cracking sound as she opened to the first page. Girlish handwriting slashed impatiently over the pages, and she realized that indeed this was a teen diary. Madeline seemed to be about sixteen or so, and she gushed about friends, boys, going to the movies and all the other stuff a girl her age would find fascinating.

With Mike leaning close enough that their shoulders brushed, they skimmed pages quickly. There were time gaps, sometimes long ones of several months, then they reached a section where Madeline gushed about her upcoming wedding, pages of details about dresses and bridesmaids and flowers.

"Who is she marrying?" Mike asked finally. "She doesn't really mention him. You'd think she'd be going on about her fiancé, too."

"Yeah." Del leaned back, giving her eyes a break. With the passage of time, Madeline's handwriting had become smaller and had lost some of its neatness. "More coffee?"

"And another pair of eyes if you have them."

"Are you reading my mind?"

"Always possible."

Then as she grinned at him, he moved in and kissed her. A gentle kiss, almost questioning. After their moments last night when only the sound of a slamming door had kept them from going much further, Del was at once surprised and touched. Surprised that he should be uncertain, touched that he thought it possible she might have changed her mind since last night.

But she hadn't. So she leaned into his kiss and looped her arm around his neck. He responded by wrapping her in a tight hug and kissing her more deeply, his tongue finding hers in a mating dance as old as time. She felt desire sink heavily to her center, a feeling so strong that it almost made her squirm with need.

Then, with obvious reluctance, he broke the kiss. His face inches from hers, he said, "I don't think this is the time or place. If a door slams again, I may become impotent for life."

The way he said it made her giggle, a sound surprisingly like Colleen's. She leaned toward him and kissed him lightly. "I can't say I blame you."

"Coffee," he repeated. "I'll get it."

And right then she absolutely hated this house. Absolutely hated whatever was wrong with it, because otherwise she'd be heading upstairs to lie down beside Mike and share lovemaking with him, something she hadn't wanted since Don died. Something she wanted more now than she could ever remember wanting it before.

Instead she had strange noises and a diary which, frankly, wasn't all that interesting.

She glanced at the wall clock above the sink as Mike poured the coffee. "I need to go help Colleen get ready for bed soon."

"Sure. Just say when. If you want, I can stay here."

"Maybe fifteen minutes." She reached for the fresh coffee and sipped it gratefully. "What's your bet on how much we learn from this diary?"

"I think we need to keep reading."

"Yeah." She sighed. "That feeling. It's still nagging at me, too."

"I'd like to point out that so far I haven't read a single thing that would require that diary to be hidden from anyone."

Del arched her brow. "So you think things changed later?"

"Most definitely. Because Madeline felt she had to hide it securely, and we're not talking about between the mattresses or beneath the socks in a drawer."

"You're right." She glanced at the clock again, feeling reenergized. "Let me go take care of Colleen right now. I'll be right back, unless you want to come over with me."

"Can I confess I've been thinking of chocolate chip cookies?"

So they went together, and she noticed that it was he who this time picked up the diary, as if reluctant to leave it in the house.

But she had changed all the window locks, and as far as she knew she and her aunt Sally were the only ones who had keys. So nobody could possibly get in, right?

Back at Mike's, they found Colleen quite ready for bed, although she was still in the midst of an animated movie. Sally was sitting in an armchair, with one of the magazines she had apparently brought with her.

Mike found the cookies and put a half dozen in a small bag, and then they headed back to her house. Once again at the kitchen table, they resumed reading.

That was when the horror began to unfold. Madeline went from thrilled about her marriage and the excitement of being a newlywed to something furtive and ugly. Bubbling with excitement gave way to terser notes, a record of being increasingly abused. Threatened, yelled at, controlled and finally beaten.

And the final note: *I'm leaving. Tomorrow. I can't hide this anymore and I don't want to. He could kill the baby! I hate him, I hate him, I hate him...*

Page after page filled with "I hate him" until there was nothing at all.

"Good God," Del whispered. "Oh, God."

Mike reached for the book and closed it. The sound seemed almost final.

They sat silently as minutes ticked by. Del felt as if she'd just been touched by a toxin so awful she wanted to wash it off. The anguish in the final entries, so few and so sparse, had hit her as hard as if she'd witnessed it all. It was as if she could mentally fill in all the gaps that Madeline had left in her tale.

Mike rubbed his eyes with thumb and forefinger, sighing heavily. "I guess," he said eventually, "that's why she hid it."

"I guess."

He leaned back in his chair, drumming his fingers absently on his thighs, staring into space.

"She wanted us to find this."

Del's gaze snapped to him. "What?"

"Don't you feel it? She wanted us to find this. For someone to know…"

Del wasn't ready to leap quite that far. "You can't know that."

"She wanted someone to know what happened to her. I feel it. Laugh at me if you want, but the house isn't quite as sad now."

Since she'd never really felt the house's sadness, she wanted to argue. Then she noticed the qualifier in what he said. "Not as sad? You mean it's still sad?"

He nodded slowly. "There's a lightening, but it's not finished."

"Hell." Del nearly snapped the word, then felt immediately awful. "Sorry. It's just…"

"Just that you can't handle my way of looking at the world."

"No!" She glared at him. "It's not that. If you want to listen to rocks, that's fine by me. My problem is that you keep saying something is wrong in this house, my daughter is scared of this house, I've started to hate the place, and I don't know how the hell to fix any of that!"

"I don't *listen* to rocks. Not the way you mean."

"You don't know what I mean, obviously, or you wouldn't be getting all offended. What I meant was, I have no problem with your *beliefs*. I have a problem with the mess I'm in, and I don't know how to fix it. I don't really know where to start. Stop hearing me through your filters. I'm open-minded. If you say the house is still sad, the house is still sad, whether I feel it or not. But damn it, I need some way to *fix* this."

"Del…"

"I don't necessarily mean fixing the house's sadness. Have you forgotten that there's good cause to believe that someone is getting in here for some reason? That there are noises I can't explain? That my tools move? And excuse me if I don't think a *house* can do all that."

She jumped up from her chair, wrapping her arms tightly around herself, and began to pace the kitchen. "What do I do? Tearing out walls isn't going to fix it. Moving out is impossible, at least at this point. As long as only Colleen and I can live in this place while it's torn up, I need to keep trying to rent the other place I just finished so I can meet my bills. Colleen doesn't want to come back here. I promised she didn't have to until I solved the problem. This is one huge heaping stinking mess!"

She reached a counter and came to an abrupt halt, leaning forward on her elbows and putting her forehead in the palms of her hands. "Damn," she whispered. "Damn, damn, damn."

"Maybe I'm not good for you."

"Oh, cut it out," she said wearily. "You've been good for me. I was all alone and now I'm not. You saved Colleen from spending another night here. You opened your home to virtual strangers, you helped me tear out walls and cart a ton of trash. If you haven't been good for me, then nobody could be."

Silence answered her. Then, amazingly, strong arms closed around her from behind and lips found the nape of her neck. A shiver trickled through her, one of pleasure. Oh, Lord, here? Now? In this house?

"Del." He murmured her name and kissed the nape of her neck again. Another thrill ran through her.

"Nothing's adding up," she whispered.

"What do you mean?"

"I'm so upset and yet I…want you. Now. Here."

"I want you, too," he said huskily. "Here. Now. I'll risk it if you will."

She straightened then, turning within the circle of his arms to look at him. Reaching up, she touched his cheek, tracing his beautiful cheekbones, tracing his wonderful lips. "Am I going crazy?" She whispered the words.

"No crazier than I am."

She felt so off-kilter from the past few days, but one thing shone through as strong and certain: she wanted him. She wanted to lie naked with this man and learn his body as well as she knew her own. She wanted to know every secret that could make him sigh or moan. She wanted to feel her body hum once again to longing and rhythms she'd abandoned four years ago.

He seemed to read her answer in her eyes. "Just be sure," he asked. "Just be very sure."

"I'm sure."

"And no matter what we hear, we ignore it."

"I'll ignore everything short of a human being walking into the room."

At that he smiled faintly and dropped a kiss on her nose, then on her lips. "The house will leave us alone tonight."

And she didn't care how he knew that. When he took her hand and guided her toward the hall and the stairway, she felt as if strength was entering every muscle. A troubled thought flickered through her mind, because he brought the diary with them. He seemed so protective of it.

But whatever compelled him to do that, she soon forgot. Standing in her bedroom, in a pool of moonlight, she watched him close and lock the bedroom door.

"Maybe," she said, "you should block it somehow." And then she laughed.

He laughed, too, and the whole mood changed. From a heaviness, in an instant they moved to a lightness, a readiness to smile as if they were embarking on a wonderful journey and could hardly wait.

He pulled her dresser over, though, so it would prevent the door from opening. "Good enough?"

She laughed again. "I defy anyone mortal to get in here."

"That's all we need then. I may have animistic tendencies, but ghosts don't scare me. They can whisper, they can talk, but they can't hurt us."

And for some reason she spread her arms and said to the house, "Give us tonight. Just tonight. I promise we'll work on finding out what happened tomorrow."

Mike stepped toward her, smiling. "That wasn't so hard, was it?"

"Ah, but will the house listen?"

"For tonight."

He kissed her again, long and deep, then stepped back. Button by button he began to open his shirt. Smiling, she felt the courage to do the same, reaching for the buttons on her work shirt. At the same moment they dropped fabric to the floor.

"You're beautiful," he murmured. "So beautiful."

"So are you."

He reached out and ran his fingertips lightly across her midriff. At once her center clenched with delight and another shiver of longing passed through her. "Oh, Mike," she whispered raggedly.

In the moonlight, half dressed, he looked like a god to her. His chest was smooth and perfectly muscled, telling her that being a vet wasn't light work.

He ran his fingers along her shoulders and down her arms.

"Can I tell you a secret?" he asked softly.

"Sure."

"I've always been drawn to women who work

hard with their bodies. Women have such beautiful musculature."

"Only a doctor could say that."

A quiet laugh escaped him. "I know some men look for softness, but for me a woman with an athletic body has always been more appealing. It's one of the first things that attracted me to you."

"I hope you like callused hands."

"Love 'em."

Then like a magician, he unhooked the front clasp of her bra and her breasts spilled free.

"Perfect," he murmured, and before she could answer, he swooped in and took one of her nipples in his mouth, sucking strongly. An instant cord of electricity ran from her womb to her core, causing a resonant throbbing that drew a groan from her.

The world tilted, and she found herself on her back on the bed. He popped the snap on her jeans and tucked them down along with her panties until they caught on her work boots.

"Oh, crap," he said, sounding amused.

"What?"

"Damn boots have laces, and right now I'm feeling ham-handed." But he dealt with that by pulling the boots off, still tied.

And then she lay naked in the moonlight while he stood over the bed, drinking her in with his eyes. "I wouldn't change one thing about you," he said.

"Not even my mind?"

"Most especially not your mind."

A kind of peace flowed through her when she heard that. They might have arguments in the future because of their different worldviews, but he didn't want to change her. She could live with that. But as soon as that feeling of peace hit, it was followed by something much less peaceful.

"Are you going to leave me here by myself?"

Another laugh escaped him, short and thickened, and he kicked away his own boots then reached for the snap on his jeans. He paused then, looking down at her.

"Quit teasing," she whispered. "Mike, quit teasing."

"I just don't want to stop looking at you."

"Try feeling me instead."

The words seemed to galvanize him. He stripped his jeans then stood for a few moments in the moonlight, giving her a chance to drink him in. "Do I meet your approval?"

"More than you can know." She thought she'd never seen a man so perfect. A man so ready for her. That gave her another delicious thrill. She held out a hand, and at once he joined her on the bed, driving the rest of the world away, replacing it with the most basic and elemental reality: that of a man and a woman coming together for the first time.

Skin against skin. Was there a more glorious feeling in the world, than two bodies joining this way? It felt to Del as if every cell of her skin responded to every brush of his from head to toe, demanding that she just let go and give in to primal need.

His lips painted her with fire, moving along her neck and then lower as her hand sought to discover him, moving over the rippling, bunching muscles of his back, then lower until they found his waist and the powerful muscles of his rump. There her hands paused, trying to grasp, trying to bring him closer still. But he wasn't yet ready to yield. Instead his lips continued their magical quest, first from one nipple to the other, sucking so strongly that her entire body responded, arching toward him, demanding fulfillment.

But even as he sucked her to a near frenzy, his hand wandered over her midriff, over her belly until it found the damp nest between her legs. There his fingers played her as if she were an instrument, stroking, teasing, promising but never delivering.

Soft moans escaped her, and a kind of delightful frustration filled her. Had she ever been ready so fast? Doubtful, but she was ready now, yet he kept her waiting, hovering on a brink that was almost scary in its height, knowing that one step, just one step, would carry her off into the chasm.

She hardly realized that her hands began to nearly claw him as she voicelessly begged for more. Her legs clamped around his hand, rocking against him, trying to find the answer she so needed.

Until finally, finally, he rose over her.

He swore. "I don't have a condom."

"I do…I do…" She knew they were old, but she didn't care. All that mattered was that nothing stopped them now. Reaching out, she fumbled at the drawer in the night table. He took over, pulling out the box, tearing open a packet as he straddled her.

Then she reached out and took the latex from him, refusing to be denied the experience of feeling him as she rolled the protection smoothly onto his staff. Loving the way he groaned at her touch. The way he threw back his head as if it was almost too much to bear.

And then he lowered himself over her, finding her breast with his mouth at the same moment he thrust into her. It was like the completing of a circuit. The thrill rocketed through her, holding her taut in its grip as he plunged, filling a long empty place, as he sucked a breast that had not nursed in too long.

With one hand she clasped the back of his head; with the other she gripped his rear, urging him on, wanting him deeper inside her than he could possibly go.

He thrust again and again, and any one of those thrusts could have pushed her over the edge, but she fought to hold the moment back, to cling to this amazing, aching, overwhelming anticipation as long as possible.

But her body betrayed her. With a cry she tumbled over the edge, and just moments later he followed her with a deep groan.

And then the house felt happy.

And sated.

With her body still clenching with aftershocks, Del clung tightly to Mike. She never wanted to let go.

Chapter 10

Morning arrived all too quickly. After a night of cuddling and lovemaking, Del didn't feel quite so much anger and dislike for the house.

But a change in her feelings didn't solve any problems. She showered quickly, changed into fresh work clothes, then took Colleen to school. Mike went off to work, promising to try to get back early again to help her.

Edgar and Jimmy showed up at eight-thirty. Edgar went to work on installing the new shower in the downstairs bath so that Del would no longer have to lift her daughter over the edge of the tub to sit in her shower chair.

"That'll save my back," she told Edgar.

"I can see how it would. I don't know how you've managed all this time, Del."

"I have a strong back, I guess." She glanced over her shoulder to see Jimmy checking all the exposed wiring in Colleen's former bedroom, using a meter to look for shorts. Then she went back to helping Edgar pull the tub out after he disconnected the plumbing.

At once Jimmy was there. "Let me do that, Ms. Del. That tub's heavy."

"Must be one of those old wrought-iron ones," Edgar grunted as he shoved. "Shame to throw it away."

"I just want to get it out to the garage," Del said. "If not today, at least we can get it out of the way for now. I figure I can probably sell it."

"Don't doubt it," was Jimmy's response as they worked on tugging the tub through the door. It took the three of them nearly a half hour to get the tub through the kitchen and to a place near the back door.

"Cripes," Edgar said, wiping his forehead with his sleeve. "Let's let it rest for now. We can move it the rest of the way later."

So it was back to work in the bathroom, this time extending plumbing up the wall to a good height for a showerhead.

"Okay," Edgar said finally after he'd welded the last copper pipe. "Let's go get the enclosure."

Del had had it delivered through the outside cellar doors so it was in the basement. She and Edgar headed down the stairs together and found Jimmy down there.

"Is something wrong?" Del asked immediately.

He shook his head. "Not sure. I'm getting low voltage on the electrical lines in the bedroom, but I can't figure out where the bleed is. And if you have a short, you should blow a fuse. You *are* going to replace this box with circuit breakers, right?"

"Of course," Del answered. "Code."

"Yeah, code." Jimmy shook his head, peering at the fuse box with a flashlight.

Del felt a tingle along her nerve endings. "Jimmy?"

He looked at her. "Yeah?"

"Could this cause a fire?"

"It's always possible. But you remember when you bought the place?"

Del nodded.

"There weren't no bleed then. And I'm not finding one in the rooms where you took out the walls. Damn." He stepped back from the fuse box, closed it and scratched his head. "I don't like this, Ms. Del."

She stood there uncertainly. "Jimmy, my strong suit isn't electricity, but how could something be causing a power drop in Colleen's room? I mean, just plugging something in for example…something that really sucks power…wouldn't that cause just a temporary drop? Like when a major appliance turns on? The way the lights dim when I first ramp up my table saw?"

"You'd think." He looked at her, shrugging.

"And a short would blow the fuse?"

"It's supposed to." He scratched his head again. "I don't like this," he repeated. "Something in the wiring ain't right. Something's bleeding power steadily, but not enough to be an outright short."

"Does that make it any less dangerous?"

"Can't say. Gotta find the problem."

"What do you suggest?"

His answer was short and to the point. "Don't sleep here."

She swore softly and turned to find Edgar just standing there, listening. Well, of course. Edgar was a plumber. This probably made just about as much sense to him as it did to her. She wasn't totally ignorant of electricity, but she couldn't for the life of her imagine how this could be happening.

"Okay," she said, looking at Jimmy again. "Try to find it. In the meantime, I'm going to help Edgar with the shower. If you need me, just holler."

Jimmy nodded and turned his flashlight back to the wiring that emerged from the fuse box, beginning to follow it along the basement ceiling in the general direction of Colleen's room.

"Oh, and Jimmy?"

"Ma'am?"

"We discussed using conduit for the new wiring, right?"

"Yup. Surely did. Beginning to think we may have to tear it all out."

"I've suspected that from the beginning. I doubt any of this would meet code."

"Likely not," he agreed.

Edgar helped her open the box containing all the parts of the new shower enclosure, then together they carried the foam-wrapped panels upstairs to Colleen's room.

She and Edgar leaned the panels carefully against the walls then made one last trip for the bottom and assorted odds and ends. During that time, Jimmy had moved back upstairs and was following a meter along a wall.

Unlike the old tub, the new shower came with a pan that sat below the enclosure's tile floor to catch any overflow and prevent water damage. Edgar attached it to the floor and then sealed any possible gaps around screws with thick, gooey caulking. Once they got the wall through which the plumbing lines would project firmly in place, the rest went swiftly.

By two, the shower was completely installed and the water was running. Edgar flashed her a grin. "Tomorrow the toilet."

Rubbing her lower back, Del leaned one shoulder against the wall. "I'm thinking about taking the fixture I bought back and exchanging it for something that would be easier for Colleen to use."

He lifted his brow. "You're not going to turn this house over like the rest?"

Good question, she thought. Good question. She had promised Colleen she wouldn't have to live here until she got rid of the noises, and she hadn't been able to find out a damn thing about the noises. Cool. Very cool.

"I don't know," she said finally. "I probably should. Either way, yeah, we can put in the new toilet tomorrow. And maybe the sink."

He nodded. "Okay. See you in the morning."

But he didn't pick up his tools, and she knew why. In this business, payment didn't wait.

He followed her into the kitchen, where she took her business checkbook out of a drawer and wrote him a draft for the day's labor.

As he was leaving, Jimmy came down from the upstairs.

"Did you find anything?" she asked.

"No." He didn't look happy. "I'm coming back in the morning. Something's wrong and I don't like it. Just don't you sleep here tonight, Ms. Del."

"I won't," she promised. She asked what she owed him and he shrugged it off.

"Ain't fixed nothin' yet," he said. Then he nodded, picked up his tools and left.

And she was alone in the house. A glance at her watch told her she needed to race to pick up Colleen. No time for even a quick wash.

Hurrying, she checked all the locks, then set out for the school.

Colleen seemed a lot happier knowing she didn't have to go back to the house. A quick call to Sally resulted in a short shopping list, so they hit the grocery. She even yielded to Colleen's pleas for some diet soda.

And by the time she got everything taken care of, it was after four and Mike still hadn't come home. Almost as soon as she thought of him, though, her cell phone rang.

"Hi, Del," Mike said. "I'm sorry, but I had an emergency. It might be an hour or more before I can get home."

"That's fine. I think I'm almost done with work for the day. I may go back and clean up a bit, though."

He paused. "Why don't you wait for me?"

"I'm just going to get some trash out. It won't take ten minutes. I'll see you soon."

There were words she wanted to say, words she wanted to hear from him, but she gathered he wasn't alone. Last night he had called her *darling,* and *sweetheart,* but over the phone she was *Del* again.

She felt a pang as she said goodbye, then told herself not to be ridiculous. Now, if he came home and didn't call her *darling* or *sweetheart,* she'd have something to wonder about.

"Sally?"

"Yes, dear?"

"I'm going over to the house to carry out some trash."

"That's fine, dear. I'll get started on dinner soon."

As she crossed the lawn, she decided to call Miss Emma at the library.

"Still haven't found a single thing about that house," Emma responded cheerfully. "Apparently nothing news-worthy ever happened there. At least nothing I've found yet."

"I can't thank you enough for looking."

"Actually, I think I'm having fun, and probably taking longer than necessary because I keep getting distracted by other stories."

Del had to laugh. "Would you like to search something else for me?"

"Sure, why not?"

"Who was Madeline James?"

"Hmm." Emma's tone grew thoughtful as Del climbed the steps and started to unlock the front door. "Now that *does* sound familiar. Did I go to high school with her?" But she apparently didn't expect an answer. "I'll look her up. Why do you need to know?"

"I found her diary."

"Oh! I bet she would love to have that back. Those things look so silly to us when we're young and look back on them, but when we get older they can be downright fascinating. I'll let you know what I find."

"Thanks, Miss Emma."

"My pleasure, Del. I've actually been having a ball."

Del wished she could say the same. Instead she headed for the basement to pick up the cardboard that had encased the shower enclosure. She could have asked

Edgar to help get rid of it, but she hadn't wanted to pay for the extra time. Pulling a utility knife from her pocket, she snapped it open and began to cut cardboard to manageable sizes.

A fire hazard because there was a power bleed somewhere in the house. That really shook her, because she'd had Jimmy check it out before she bought the place. She'd been worried about the wiring from the start, given the place was so old. And while she might expose Colleen to the dust and mess of renovation, she would *not* expose her daughter to a dangerous dwelling. She'd had the building inspector in, and Edgar and Jimmy both before she'd even made an offer. No one had thought the place dangerous *then*.

She had guessed she would probably need to replace the wiring, given the age of the place and the fact that she was bound to do damage tearing out the rotten walls, but to learn she had a voltage drop in Colleen's room, something which Jimmy couldn't locate, seriously troubled her.

As she cut cardboard and stacked it neatly, she tried to remember anything she might have done to cause the problem. The only trouble with that, of course, was that Jimmy should have found the bleed easily enough in the walls she'd already torn out.

So what else was there?

She went back to the fuse box, opened it and studied it with the help of a penlight she always carried in the breast pocket of her work shirt. Maybe there was something wrong with it. Well, there had to be, didn't there? She couldn't imagine how she could have a power bleed somewhere without blowing a fuse. The very idea struck her as counterintuitive.

When the refrigerator compressor came on, the lights dimmed just briefly until the current draw leveled out again. It happened fast, something she almost didn't notice. So how could you have a persistent bleed that wouldn't be compensated for unless you had a major short, one that should blow a fuse?

All the fuses looked okay, as they should considering she had put in fresh ones when they moved in.

She squatted, flashlight in hand, staring up at the fuse box as she tried to remember her all-too-brief studies in wiring and electricity years ago.

What could create a persistent power drop that couldn't be compensated for? Some kind of resistor?

Yeah, a resistor. But they made heat, which was how they expended the energy they pulled out of the system. Light and heat, just like a lightbulb.

Well, how could something like that have happened all of a sudden and all on its own?

She knew she should wait for Jimmy to come back in the morning. He was the expert, after all, the one with the license and years of experience.

But she hated problems she couldn't solve.

Straightening, she started to follow the wiring from the fuse box, just as Jimmy had. Not that she really expected to see anything. If it was obvious, Jimmy would have found it.

Walking slowly, she peered up at the wires. They all were insulated, and she didn't see any breaks in the insulation. A couple had been capped off with plastic, having been cut and thrown into disuse. A couple headed for the overhead bulb fixtures that were attached to the overhead joists, and which cast little enough light in the basement.

Everything looked absolutely normal, and she was just about to give up when her flashlight trailed across one wire.

It went *behind* the brick wall.

Her opinion of the person who put up that wall sank another notch lower. Not only lousy mortar that was crumbling, but unevenly laid bricks, too. And now, apparently, the builder had just sealed up an outlet box. Stupid.

She considered cutting and capping the wire right then and there and couldn't understand why the guy who had built the wall hadn't done it himself. If water got in there…

Sighing, she traced the wire back to the fuse box and tried to determine which fuse it was attached to. Well, of course, the basement fuse. She'd have to turn out all the lights down here if she wanted to cut that one wire.

Shoot.

Well, it had survived this long.

She shoved her knife back into her pocket and pulled out her cell phone to call Sally and tell her she'd be over in a few minutes, that she just wanted to take care of a bit of business first. Like tearing down enough of that wall to see where the wire went. As crumbly as the mortar was, the only thing she needed to fear was carelessness.

But just before she could flip her phone open, it rang.

"Hi," said the voice of Emma Dalton, the librarian. "I found Madeline James!"

"Really? Where is she?"

"Well, that's the thing. She left town about fifteen

years ago, and other than a couple of postcards she sent to her husband and friends, nobody's heard from her."

"Nobody? No family?"

"Her parents died right after she got married. And then after about two years, she took off. The story is she couldn't stand life around here anymore, that she wanted more adventure and more money. She was certainly pretty enough to marry it."

"But…" Del's mind balked. "That's weird."

"Well," said Emma, lowering her voice a bit, "I was thinking that, too. Jimmy reported her missing about two days after she left, and then a week later he got a postcard, so they stopped looking for her."

Del's heart seemed to stop. "Jimmy? Jimmy who?"

"Jimmy Morton."

Her neck prickled. Del turned slowly and looked at the brick wall, dark and ugly in the light from two sixty-watt bulbs. "Jimmy Morton, as in the electrician?"

"The same. He divorced her about a year later, but they couldn't even find her to deliver the notice to. Not the first time this has happened."

"I'm sure." Del hesitated, a chill creeping along her spine even as her mind refused the thoughts that were trying to surge to awareness. "Did anybody else ever hear from her?"

"According to the report I read, two of her best friends got cards, too. Hold on, it's in one of these old police reports."

Del waited patiently until she heard a rustle as Emma came back on the line. "Yes. Several of her friends received postcards, too. It seems she'd been thinking of leaving Jimmy for a while, so none of them were surprised. Anyway, the report said they verified the handwriting was hers, so no question of abduction or anything like that. The girl simply kicked up her heels and left."

"Well, her diary said she was going to leave."

"A shame we can't get it to her. She'd probably look back at it now and laugh."

I doubt it, Del thought as she said goodbye to Emma.

So Jimmy had lived in this house once, with his wife. Odd that he'd never mentioned it.

Or maybe not so odd. Why would he want to bring up such a humiliating, painful memory?

Stop it, she told herself. Cripes, why was her imagination running away from her? The woman had said in her diary she was leaving. She'd told her friends she was leaving. She'd sent postcards from wherever she'd gone, and her friends said it was her handwriting.

So no mystery, right?

"Right," she said aloud to the empty basement.

Except there was a mystery *now.* A mystery with the electrical power, a mystery with strange noises, and Jimmy himself who had said it wouldn't be safe to stay in the house until he found the electrical problem.

An electrical problem that made no sense whatever to her unless someone had created it. Or invented it.

Her phone rang again, jarring her, and she looked at it. Mike. "Hello?"

"Hi, sweetie." Apparently he was alone now, and the endearment made her smile. "I'm still hung up, but not for much longer, I promise."

"What happened?"

"Dog meets car. As usual, the dog took the worst of it."

"Will it be all right?"

"I'm pretty sure, but we had to do some extensive surgery and I'm going to help clean up. I'm also waiting for one of my assistants to come in to watch the poor guy overnight. Forty-five minutes. Maybe an hour. Tell Sally I'm sorry, if she made dinner."

"She did. I'll tell her. She'll understand, Mike."

"I hope so. Be there just as soon as I can."

She disconnected and called Sally to let her know.

"Not a problem," Sally answered. "Casseroles keep well. When are you coming back?"

"I just need to check something. Is Colleen okay?"

"She's doing just fine. She did ask for that LMNO music thing of hers."

"Her MP3 player. Tell her I'll bring it. I can't believe I forgot to get it for her yesterday."

"She'll live. She's watching some comedy reruns right now."

Del's cell began to beep. "Sally, my phone's dying. Be there as soon as I can."

She shut the phone, turned it off to save the last of the battery and shoved it into her pocket. *Okay, get the cardboard out, go clean up for dinner and wait for Mike.*

Except she no sooner reached the foot of the basement stairs when her neck started prickling again.

Was this what Mike meant when he said the house felt sad to him? Or was it something else?

She turned slowly, looking around the basement, seeing absolutely nothing except some tools, ladders, the stack of cardboard she'd just made and a couple of boxes holding bathroom fixtures she intended to install tomorrow.

An empty room that certainly didn't feel empty.

And a brick wall that made absolutely no sense.

No, she wasn't going to start *that* job tonight.

Oh, yes, she was.

Okay, just around the wire, just to see if maybe it was capped off right behind the brick. That much she could justify. If there was any place in this house that could have an electrical drain that Jimmy hadn't noticed during his first inspection, that would be it. After all, it had rained a lot over the past few days. Something back there might be damp.

Picking up a hammer and chisel, she dragged a stepladder over to that end of the wall. She could have reached the top bricks while standing on the floor, but she didn't want to risk the possibility of bricks falling on her head when the mortar crumbled.

Just before she struck the first blow, she had a thought. More light would be useful. Very useful.

Sighing, she climbed down and went back upstairs to get a couple of her work lights. Back in the basement, she hung them to the side on nails in the rafters so they were in a position not to blind her as she looked at the bricks.

The first brick came loose with one blow of the hammer against the chisel. Not caring if she damaged it, she tossed it to the floor, where it made a surprisingly high-pitched *thunk* as it hit the cement.

Bricks, she had noted over the years, had different voices according to how dense they were and the amount of firing they'd received. Differences in quality made for differences in voices.

She scraped the remaining mortar away and saw that the wire continued to run behind the bricks.

Great. She touched the basement wall behind and felt a definite dampness. This wall absolutely had to go.

But she also felt a shuddering wave of relief. The thought she had refused to entertain just a short while ago while speaking with Emma surged up along with the relief. Nothing was hidden behind that wall. Nothing. There was no room. The brick she had removed had rested flat against the cement wall behind it.

Feeling almost weak with relief, she leaned against the ladder and put her head down for a moment. How could she have even suspected such a thing? Too many TV shows, she decided. Too damn many.

She was appalled that her own mind had even dredged up such a notion, particularly about a man she had worked with over the past several years. One who seemed nice.

God! She lifted her head, telling herself to just head back to Mike's and enjoy a nice dinner.

And that was when she saw it. Looking along the length of the wall for the first time, perhaps aided by the work lights she had hung, she saw a definite bulge in the brick wall. Not huge, but as if something were pressing on it, working it slowly away from the wall behind.

It was not big enough to conceal anything, but she was curious anyway. Climbing down from the ladder, she used her hammer, tapping gently along the wall, listening to the sounds. And when she got to the bulge, those sounds changed. Deadened.

There was definitely something different back there.

She tried rationalizing. Maybe someone had put this wall in because part of the basement wall had given way.

But that didn't make sense. As a repair job for that kind of problem, this was a terrible idea. Bricks just didn't offer the same kind of strength. Even a well-mortared cinderblock wall with reinforcing rods would have been within the scope of a home handyman.

Of course, during her renovation career, she'd found a whole lot of really strange repair jobs.

Sighing, she tapped the wall again and heard that deadened sound. Why did she think this was going to turn into one helluva repair job?

She laid the palm of her hand against the bulging bricks and felt dampness. Water was definitely getting in.

And if water was seeping upward into the exterior wall, then she had truly big trouble on her hands.

Feeling suddenly frustrated, she banged her hammer hard against the bulge. A brick cracked. She banged again, determined to know what she was up against here.

Three more bangs and some of the bricks broke enough that she could pry them out with her hammer's claw, and then she dropped her hammer to work with her fingers. At once she found wet mud.

"Holy hell," she muttered. She pushed her hand in a bit farther and felt tree roots, more mud, something hard and pitted. "What the…?"

Water began to trickle out of the mud.

"You shouldn't have done that."

Startled, she fell to her hands and knees, then looked around to see Jimmy. "What are you doing here?" she asked, confused by his sudden appearance. "I thought you were coming back in the morning."

"I told you not to sleep here tonight."

The prickling on the back of her neck reached an uncomfortable level. "I'm not going to," she said. And Jimmy looked...odd. Not like himself.

"That wall could fall on you now," he said.

She glanced at it and realized he was right. Pulling out those bricks had destabilized it, and water was coming through the opening even faster now.

"I'll brace it," she said. "In the morning we can rip it out. There's a hole in the concrete behind it."

"I know."

That was the moment when the prickling turned to a chill. Trying to be furtive, she felt around for her hammer. Damn it, where had it gone?

"It'll be such a tragedy when they find you tomorrow," he said.

"Tragedy?" Her heart was racing like a horse's at the end of a derby. "Why should there be a tragedy?" Although now she knew, absolutely knew, that her imagination hadn't run away with her.

"Buried under that brick wall you should never have tried to take down by yourself."

She poised herself, ready to spring. But before she could reach her feet, Jimmy ran at her carrying her sledgehammer.

Oh, God! Somehow she managed to shove herself away from the wall just before Jimmy hit her. He hit the wall himself, and more bricks cracked.

But it gave her time, just enough time to get to her feet. "Jimmy," she said, pretending she knew nothing, "what's wrong with you?"

A weapon. She needed a weapon. Some way to protect herself from that sledgehammer. Some way to knock it out of his hands. Fast. She'd have to move fast.

All she had was a utility knife. And her hammer...
She looked away from him just long enough to locate
it. Out of reach, at least right now.

But he wanted her to be buried under bricks. So if
she started to swing around in a way that would bring
her back to the wall...

She edged carefully, circling. He followed her,
something at once intent and vacant in his gaze. A quick
glance at the floor told her that she might be able to get
him to the wet spot that was growing as water trickled
through the hole in the wall.

A wet spot that would be as slippery as ice, as she
knew from experience. This floor in this basement had
never been roughened. At some time or other, it had
been covered with a smooth concrete coat. Perhaps with
intent to paint it.

All that mattered was that she might be able to get
him to slip in that water.

Taking a huge risk when she judged the time right,
she jumped toward him. Instinctively he leaped back
and hit the water. His feet slipped and he struggled for
balance.

Del kept right on charging, head lowered until she
butted him in the chest. She heard the sledgehammer
fall.

And then she was on the floor, rolling around with
Jimmy as he punched at her and then tried to get his
hands around her throat.

But hard work had made her strong. She shoved her
forearms up between Jimmy's arms and snapped them
outward with enough strength that although she didn't
have the leverage to break his grip, he loosened it.

She drew a deep breath then turned her head and bit him as hard as she could on his wrist.

He yelped and let go, instinctively pulling away from the pain. It was enough to allow her to shove at him and try to wiggle from beneath him.

She almost made it, then he came back at her, more enraged than ever.

Damn, she thought wildly, falling hadn't been a good idea. She couldn't get leverage anywhere on her back. But then she realized one of his legs had fallen between hers. Gasping another deep breath, she yanked her knee upward as hard as she could manage.

Jimmy howled and reared away from that awful pain. Struggling, Del managed to roll over, her hands clawing to find the hammer she'd dropped.

She heard the scrape of the sledgehammer and knew Jimmy, nearly paralyzed with pain as he must be, had found his weapon again. Panic nearly swamped her, adding to her strength. She managed with a single shove to yank her legs from beneath him.

If she could just get to her feet before he did, before he got enough leverage to use that sledgehammer...

Oh, God, she had to get out of this. Who would take care of Colleen?

Rage joined fear as fuel as she thought of her daughter. Scrambling, she got her feet beneath her, her gaze fixed on Jimmy, who was rising again, hammer in hand.

Damn! She thought wildly, trying to weigh options, realizing that one blow of that sledgehammer would put her down.

"Del?" The call seemed to come from far away. It sounded like Mike, but it was too soon for Mike. Feeling like a threatened animal, she watched Jimmy straighten and realized there was only one thing she could do.

With her legs still bent, her feet beneath her, she sprang at his knees, hitting him with her shoulder right at the kneecaps.

And hit him hard. She lost her wind at the impact when she landed on her stomach. Her shoulder hurt almost as if it had been broken.

But now Jimmy was on the floor again, on his back, unable to use that sledgehammer to any real purpose.

Stand, she ordered herself. *Stand.* But she couldn't catch her breath. Her body seemed almost paralyzed. And Jimmy had started to move again.

God, why couldn't she breathe?

Then, the most welcome sound in the world.

"Del? Del!"

The thudding of footsteps on the wooden stairs. With a great gulp she finally gasped for air, and her limbs began to move again.

And Jimmy reared up to his feet, staggering a little as he tried to lift the sledgehammer.

And then the most beautiful sight in the world.

Mike came flying by like a defensive end to make a rushing tackle. Like someone who had played the game and knew exactly how to do it.

Jimmy fell backward again, with an *oof* as the wind was driven from him, and this time his head cracked on the concrete.

And suddenly, unbelievably, everything went still.

Chapter 11

"Del? Del? Oh, God, honey, open your eyes!"

Had she passed out? She didn't think so. Groaning, she opened her eyes and realized she was facedown on cold concrete. She started to roll over, but Mike stopped her.

"Wait," he said. "You might be injured."

"My shoulder hurts," she mumbled and kept turning over anyway, grimacing, but pretty certain she was just bruised. "Jimmy?"

"He's out like a light. But it won't last. Cops are coming. Just don't move. I need to be sure he doesn't get up again."

"You were wonderful," she said hazily. "Great tackle."

"I played a little in college. My God, what was going on here?"

"I'm not really sure. He attacked me."

"I could see that."

Mike moved away from her as another groan sounded in the basement.

Del lay staring up at the ceiling joists, coming down from the adrenaline, feeling weak and shaky. But when she heard the scrape of metal on concrete, she stiffened. "Mike?" Another wave of panic.

"It's okay," she heard him say. "If he moves I'm gonna use this hammer on his head."

"Oh." Why did she feel so woozy? Seconds ago she'd been more focused than almost any time in her life, focused on survival. Now she felt as if she couldn't collect her thoughts.

"The cops," she said.

"I already called them."

Wow, she must have blacked out for a minute or so. Moving carefully, she felt her head, but found only the lump from falling against the bed. "Did I pass out?"

"I'm not sure. You weren't responsive for a little while there."

"I got winded when I hit the floor."

"Or maybe the pain put you out for a short while."

After what she'd just been through, anything was possible, she thought. Shock. Pain. Lack of oxygen from her fall.

A shudder passed through her and she winced as her shoulder screamed. The compulsion to get up off the cold, hard concrete was overwhelming, though, and she managed to push herself into a sitting position.

"I'm not sure you should get up," Mike said.

"I need to." She scooted over to the wall so she could sit leaning against it. Away from the brick wall where a steady stream of muddy water kept pouring onto the floor.

Then, in the distance, she heard sirens. And finally the thud of footsteps upstairs. Moments later three deputies burst into the room: Sarah Ironheart, Micah Parish and Virgil Beauregard. All of them people she knew, for which she was intensely grateful.

"Well, hell," Micah said, taking in the scene. "What happened?"

"Jimmy attacked me," Del said. "And I think you'll find his ex-wife behind that brick wall." She lifted a hand to point. "Will someone please tell Colleen and my aunt that I'm okay?"

Then she closed her eyes and leaned her head back. She was done. Finished. Kaput.

"How did you figure that all out?" Mike asked as he sat beside Del's gurney in the emergency room. X-rays had shown no broken shoulder, but she was waiting for a sling for her arm because it had become so painful to move.

"Yeah," said a familiar voice. "I want to know, too."

Del turned her head to see Gage Dalton, the county's sheriff, in the doorway. "Hi, Gage."

"How are you feeling?"

"I'm going to be fine as soon as they immobilize this arm. Did you guys find anything?"

"Plenty. We found remains behind that wall. Sorry, your basement looks like a bomb exploded. I'll make sure the county cleans it up once we're done with the scene."

Del let her head fall back on the pillow and sighed.

"I guess I'm homeless for a while now. Unless I move back into the other place."

"Move into mine," Mike suggested. "Aunt Sally can go home then, and you can have my bedroom."

Del figured she liked that idea a whole lot more than she should.

"So," Mike repeated, "now we both want to know how you figured out there was a body behind that wall."

"Thank Emma," Del said, looking at Gage. Emma was his wife. "I asked her to do some research for me. Mike and I found a diary belonging to Madeline James, and Emma was kind enough to look into it. She called me just before Jimmy attacked me, to tell me that Madeline had been married to Jimmy and that she left town fifteen years ago. Except for a few postcards right after she left, nobody heard from her."

Gage nodded. "Guess I need to question my own wife a bit."

Del managed a weary smile. "Anyway, that brick wall had been bothering me for a long time. And Jimmy claimed we had to stay out of the house because there was some kind of electrical problem. Only after he left, I couldn't figure out how such a problem would have developed, especially since there hadn't been one when we moved in, so I started looking around. I saw a wire running behind that brick wall, which bothered me because it might get damp behind there, and I pulled out a brick to follow the wire. The cement wall behind was damp, which meant water was getting in somehow, and then I saw the bulge in the wall, pulled out a few bricks, found dirt and water… But I'm running on. I admit I'd already had the ugly thought that maybe Madeline hadn't just disappeared. And then Jimmy attacked me, and it was the only way I could put the pieces together."

Gage nodded. "Jimmy admitted it. He's been trying to scare you out of that house since you mentioned you were going to get rid of that wall."

"Really?" Del felt appalled by the whole thing. "That man scared my daughter with creepy noises?" She started to sit up, furious, but Mike gently pushed her back.

"Easy," he said. "Easy."

"I don't know about noises," Gage replied. "He did say he kept moving things around when you weren't there, trying to make you feel unsafe."

"All he did was make me think I was getting forgetful. It was the damn noises that brought everything to a head. How in the world did he make them?"

"I don't know," Gage said. "Maybe he didn't, but I'll be sure to ask."

Del sighed and felt an infinite wave of weary sorrow wash over her. "No wonder the house felt sad."

Gage didn't reply directly to that crazy-sounding statement, but Mike smiled faintly at her.

"So you found Madeline?" she asked.

"Yep. We certainly did. And Jimmy admitted it. Seems he found some postcards she'd written, apparently meaning to send them just as she was leaving town. So he knew she was going, and he got furious and beat her to death."

"My God!"

"Well, I don't know if he meant to kill her. But one way or another, he did."

"He was beating her for a long time. I'll give you her diary."

"That'll be helpful." Gage shook his head. "Anyway, when the deed was done, he panicked, hammered a hole in the basement wall, buried her, then put up the bricks. And he used the postcards she'd written, mailing them from Laramie, to cover."

Del shuddered, then winced as her shoulder hurt. "That's so ugly. I never would have imagined Jimmy could do such things. At least not until tonight. But I still want to know how he made those sounds."

Gage leaned against the door frame and folded his arms. "What sounds?"

"Scratching inside the walls. Doors slamming when no door slammed."

"I can't imagine," Gage said. "If he used some kind of sound system, you'll find it when you tear out walls, won't you?"

"I guess. But I still want him to admit it."

"I'll see what I can do. And I'll try to clear out your house as soon as possible, but it might be a couple of days."

Del closed her eyes for a moment. "I don't know if I want to live there anymore. My God, a woman was buried in my basement!"

"But she'll rest now," Mike said quietly.

Del looked at him and something in her heart, in her perceptions, shifted. "Yes," she said finally. "She can rest now."

And maybe that was the most important thing.

The sun was up when Mike took her home. Colleen was waiting impatiently and demanding to stay home from school. Sally, oddly enough, had packed her battered suitcase and announced she was no longer needed.

Del hesitated. And Mike took charge.

"You're going to school, Colleen. Your mother can't lift you right now, but I can, so we'll skip your shower this once and I'll drive you to school. And take Aunt Sally home."

Sally didn't twitch a muscle, but remarked, "I put fresh sheets on your bed, Mike." It was only as she headed for the door that she gave Del a knowing wink.

Del was too weary to pay any attention. After last night, running on absolutely no sleep, she couldn't deal with anything more, even something as silly as a wink from Sally.

The shower might be impossible at the moment, but Del still had one good arm, and it was enough to help Colleen get dressed.

But Colleen reached out and gripped her forearm, stopping her. "Mom?"

"Yes, honey?"

"You're really okay?"

"Just some bruises."

Colleen slipped an arm up around her neck, and they hugged. "Mom?" she whispered.

"Yes, honey?"

"Don't…don't go away like Daddy did."

Del lost it. She started sobbing, and she hugged her daughter as tightly as she could with one arm. "I'm safe," she whispered brokenly. "I'm safe and I'm not going anywhere. I'll be right here when you come home from school. I promise."

"The bad guy is in jail, right?"

"Right. And Mike will protect me just like he did last

night." It was a rash promise, one she wasn't entitled to make, but it seemed necessary.

But then she heard a sound and looked over Colleen's head to see Mike standing there. She could have sworn his eyes seemed a little damp. "I'll protect your mom," he said to Colleen. "I promise."

He took Colleen to school and then drove Sally home, and it seemed to Del to take forever. She was exhausted, she hurt and, by God, she didn't want to be alone.

Although if she were honest, she wasn't really alone. There were enough cops swarming over her house right next door that help could have arrived in an instant.

But life had taken too much from her, and after last night she wondered if she would ever feel safe again.

But then Mike walked through the door and she realized she could. And would. At least with him.

He scooped her up and sat on the couch with her on his lap. He showered kisses all over her face. She answered eagerly, needily, knowing deep within that this was a man she didn't want to lose.

Yet she had absolutely no reason to think he wanted her in the same way. Her heart squeezed as she remembered all his objections to getting involved with a white woman. And she couldn't blame him for that. Everyone learned lessons, and lessons learned the hard way stayed the longest.

Mike's cell phone rang. He swore. "Dammit, if this is work I'm going to…" He didn't complete the thought as he fished his phone out of his breast pocket.

Del's heart sank. Of course this was a workday for him. He probably had all kinds of appointments. Should probably, in fact, be at the office right now.

The thought of spending the day without him, all

alone with nothing to think about except what had happened last night and how much she missed him, nearly scared her.

"The sheriff," he said, looking at the screen on his phone. He flipped it open and spoke. "Howdy, Gage. What's up?"

He listened for a while, then said, "Okay, I'll tell her."

"Tell me what?" she demanded as he tucked his phone away.

"Jimmy denies all knowledge of sounds in the house. And since he's admitted to everything else…" He let the sentence dangle unfinished.

Del closed her eyes, trying to absorb it. "Maybe…"

"Maybe," Mike said. "Maybe. Some things just never get answers, Del. Never."

She met his gaze. "Tell me. Do *you* think it was Madeline?"

"I don't know. But in my world that's possible. Can you live with that?"

She put her fingers to her forehead, thoughts scrambling around inside her head like worried mice, escaping every effort to grasp them. And then she knew, absolutely knew, something deep inside herself.

"If…if it was Madeline, we'll never know."

"No," he agreed.

"But if I were her, I'd sure want somebody to discover what happened to me."

"I would, too."

She drew a deep breath, then let it go. "I guess I can live with that mystery."

"Mysteries can be good things. They help remind us of the magic in life. That we don't know everything."

She nodded, accepting it. "I can deal with that."

"Then there's something else I'd like you to deal with."

She raised her eyes to his, found them dark, warm and inviting. Such beautiful eyes. "What's that?"

"I realized something last night when I came charging down those steps and saw you in so much danger. Hurt and not even moving."

"What's that?"

"I think I love you, Del. Because right then, when I thought you might be gone, I realized I didn't want to face this morning without you."

She caught her breath. All weariness vanished, replaced by a dawning of joy she had thought she would never know again. "Oh, Mike!"

"I realize we've hardly had a chance to know each other. I mean, a handful of days is hardly a courtship. But I want to take it slow. I want to date you. I want to be sure Colleen wants me around all the time. And then… and then, assuming you start to feel the same way about me, and everything's okay by Colleen, I want to marry you. Because honest to God, Del, I faced life without you last night, and it's just not worth living."

For a few moments she couldn't even find her voice. Her heart pounded wildly and a tear rolled down her cheek.

"Oh, hell," he whispered. "I made you cry. It's okay. Forget I said anything."

"No." It came out as a gasp, but then again, more strongly. "No. I won't forget. Because I want the same thing, too, Mike. The very same thing. I think I love you."

The smile on his face was beautiful. She'd always

found him beautiful, but right now he gave new meaning to the word. That gorgeous smile. She couldn't imagine a day without it.

Still smiling, he scooped her up and carried her carefully to his bedroom, where he laid her gently down.

"We'll sleep now," he whispered. He lay beside her and drew her carefully into his arms. "Then we'll wake up together and go get Colleen. Which is the way I want to wake up every single day for the rest of my life."

She couldn't think of a better future. Snuggling in, she smiled and closed her eyes.

Happiness had found her once again.

* * * * *

COMING NEXT MONTH

Available February 22, 2011

#1647 OPERATION: FORBIDDEN
Black Jaguar Squadron
Lindsay McKenna

#1648 SPECIAL AGENT'S SURRENDER
Lawmen of Black Rock
Carla Cassidy

#1649 SOLDIER'S NIGHT MISSION
H.O.T. Watch
Cindy Dees

#1650 THE DOCTOR'S DEADLY AFFAIR
Stephanie Doyle

SRSCNM0211

REQUEST YOUR FREE BOOKS!

2 FREE NOVELS
PLUS
2 FREE GIFTS!

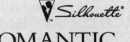

Silhouette®

ROMANTIC
SUSPENSE

Sparked by Danger, Fueled by Passion.

YES! Please send me 2 FREE Silhouette® Romantic Suspense novels and my 2 FREE gifts (gifts are worth about $10). After receiving them, if I don't wish to receive any more books, I can return the shipping statement marked "cancel." If I don't cancel, I will receive 4 brand-new novels every month and be billed just $4.24 per book in the U.S. or $4.99 per book in Canada. That's a saving of at least 15% off the cover price! It's quite a bargain! Shipping and handling is just 50¢ per book in the U.S. and 75¢ per book in Canada.* I understand that accepting the 2 free books and gifts places me under no obligation to buy anything. I can always return a shipment and cancel at any time. Even if I never buy another book, the two free books and gifts are mine to keep forever.

240/340 SDN FC95

Name _____ (PLEASE PRINT) _____

Address _____ Apt. # _____

City _____ State/Prov. _____ Zip/Postal Code _____

Signature (if under 18, a parent or guardian must sign)

Mail to the **Reader Service:**

IN U.S.A.: P.O. Box 1867, Buffalo, NY 14240-1867
IN CANADA: P.O. Box 609, Fort Erie, Ontario L2A 5X3

Not valid for current subscribers to Silhouette Romantic Suspense books.

Want to try two free books from another line?
Call 1-800-873-8635 or visit www.ReaderService.com.

* Terms and prices subject to change without notice. Prices do not include applicable taxes. Sales tax applicable in N.Y. Canadian residents will be charged applicable taxes. Offer not valid in Quebec. This offer is limited to one order per household. All orders subject to credit approval. Credit or debit balances in a customer's account(s) may be offset by any other outstanding balance owed by or to the customer. Please allow 4 to 6 weeks for delivery. Offer available while quantities last.

Your Privacy—The Reader Service is committed to protecting your privacy. Our Privacy Policy is available online at www.ReaderService.com or upon request from the Reader Service.

We make a portion of our mailing list available to reputable third parties that offer products we believe may interest you. If you prefer that we not exchange your name with third parties, or if you wish to clarify or modify your communication preferences, please visit us at www.ReaderService.com/consumerchoice or write to us at Reader Service Preference Service, P.O. Box 9062, Buffalo, NY 14269. Include your complete name and address.

SRSI1

USA TODAY *bestselling author Lynne Graham*
is back with a thrilling new trilogy
SECRETLY PREGNANT, CONVENIENTLY WED

Three heroines must marry alpha males to keep
their dreams...but Alejandro, Angelo and Cesario
are not about to be tamed!

Book 1—JEMIMA'S SECRET
Available March 2011 from Harlequin Presents®.

JEMIMA yanked open a drawer in the sideboard to find
Alfie's birth certificate. Her son was her husband's child.
It was a question of telling the truth whether she liked it or
not. She extended the certificate to Alejandro.

"This has to be nonsense," Alejandro asserted.

"Well, if you can find some other way of explaining how
I managed to give birth by that date and Alfie not be yours,
I'd like to hear it," Jemima challenged.

Alejandro glanced up, golden eyes bright as blades and
as dangerous. "All this proves is that you must still have
been pregnant when you walked out on our marriage. It
does not automatically follow that the child is mine."

"'I know it doesn't suit you to hear this news now and I
really didn't want to tell you. But I can't lie to you about it.
Someday Alfie may want to look you up and get acquainted."

"If what you have just told me is the truth, if that little
boy does prove to be mine, it was vindictive and extremely
selfish of you to leave me in ignorance!"

Jemima paled. "When I left you, I had no idea that I was
still pregnant."

"Two years is a long period of time, yet you made no
attempt to inform me that I might be a father. I will want
DNA tests to confirm your claim before I make any deci-

sion about what I want to do."

"Do as you like," she told him curtly. "*I* know who Alfie's father is and there has never been any doubt of his identity."

"I will make arrangements for the tests to be carried out and I will see you again when the result is available," Alejandro drawled with lashings of dark Spanish masculine reserve.

"I'll contact a solicitor and start the divorce," Jemima proffered in turn.

Alejandro's eyes narrowed in a piercing scrutiny that made her uncomfortable. "It would be foolish to do anything before we have that DNA result."

"I disagree," Jemima flashed back. "I should have applied for a divorce the minute I left you!"

Alejandro quirked an ebony brow. "And why didn't you?"

Jemima dealt him a fulminating glance but said nothing, merely moving past him to open her front door in a blunt invitation for him to leave.

"I'll be in touch," he delivered on the doorstep.

What is Alejandro's next move? Perhaps rekindling their marriage is the only solution! But will Jemima agree?

Find out in Lynne Graham's exciting new romance
JEMIMA'S SECRET

Available March 2011 from Harlequin Presents®.

Start your Best Body today with these top 3 nutrition tips!

1. **SHOP THE PERIMETER OF THE GROCERY STORE:** The good stuff—fruits, veggies, lean proteins and dairy—always line the outer edges of the store. When you veer into the center aisles, you enter the temptation zone, where the unhealthy foods live.

2. **WATCH PORTION SIZES:** Most portion sizes in restaurants are nearly twice the size of a true serving and at home, it's easy to "clean your plate." Use these easy serving guidelines:
   - Protein: the palm of your hand
   - Grains or Fruit: a cup of your hand
   - Veggies: the palm of two open hands

3. **USE THE RAINBOW RULE FOR PRODUCE:** Your produce drawers should be filled with every color of fruits and vegetables. The greater the variety, the more vitamins and other nutrients you add to your diet.

Find these and many more helpful tips in

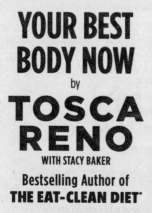

YOUR BEST BODY NOW
by
TOSCA RENO
WITH STACY BAKER
Bestselling Author of
THE EAT-CLEAN DIET®

Available wherever books are sold!

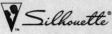